D1594129

Everlasting

Everlasting

Kelly Aul

Scripture quotations are from the King James Version of the Bible

Printed in the United States of America

ISBN   978-0692330319

Dress made by Matti's Millinery & Costumes

Making Your Costume Dreams Come True!
www.mattionline.com

BOOKS *by* KELLY AUL

NEVER FORSAKEN

Special thanks to:

- ❖ My loving family, for their hard work and amazing support.

- ❖ My dear friends, for your kind words and encouragement.

- ❖ Hannah Wagner and Matti Wangerin, for making the cover come to life with your dresses.

Most importantly, I give all the glory to my Heavenly Father, my Lord and Savior, Jesus Christ, and the precious leading of the Holy Spirit.

"The LORD has appeared of old to me, *saying:* 'Yes, I have loved you with an everlasting love; Therefore with lovingkindness I have drawn you.'"

Jeremiah 31:3

PROLOGUE

Ireland   *August 1788*

ot ya! Garrick spotted the red fox amongst the brush. He and his trusted hounds had been carefully tracking it for the past hour. Just a moment ago it seemed as though they had lost it, however, the hounds suddenly took off through the thick trees, leaving Garrick atop his horse. He was about to catch up with them when he heard a noise to his left. It was then he saw the fox.

I'll have to go it alone without the hounds. He slowly slipped the rifle from his saddle. *This shot will be easy enough. Looks like I don't need Marden's help as he thinks. I can do it without him.* Garrick finished getting his rifle ready as quietly as he could then lifted it up to his eye to aim. *What does he know anyway? He is a lousy hunter,* Garrick's prideful thoughts continued. He had never really liked his stepfather much less submit to his way of doing things.

Garrick pulled the trigger. The next thing he knew, he was lying on the ground on his back. Garrick instantly sat up to see what had taken place. As best as he could figure, the fox had made a dash towards him instead of running away from him in its frightened state, and startled his horse, sending him flying. His gun never reached its intended target. Garrick angrily got to his feet and wiped himself off just as a frightening sound was heard. It sounded like someone groaning.

Did I wound the animal after all? He looked around him as dread slowly washed over him. He heard a shriek, followed by alarming cries coming from the other side of the wooded area. It came from where his gun had been aimed only moments ago.

"Help! Someone help!" Garrick rushed through the trees and brush to a small clearing. There, in the shaded spot he found the worst. Marden lied on the ground with his son kneeling next to him. Garrick had shot his own stepfather.

"Garrick!" Reid gazed up at him through his tears.

"I...I...didn't mean to. I swear." Garrick felt numb all over. He tried to think straight. "I'll get help," he turned to leave when Marden spoke.

"There's no time," his voice was hoarse and he slowly spoke between painful breaths. Reid's sobs grew louder at this. "It's all right, son...it will be all right," Marden gasped and took hold of his son's small hand, "You must promise me."

"Anything," Reid cried. Garrick could only watch from where he stood.

"Promise me that you'll continue on with my work...it's important."

"I will," Reid promised solemnly. Though he didn't know much of what he spoke of, being only a boy of seven, he purposed to find out.

"I love you, son...see you soon......"

June 1799

Even now, more than ten years later, Garrick recalled that day as if it was yesterday. He regretted the outcome of his mistake, yet to this day, he'd never truly been sorry or even missed Marden.

Reid had just become eighteen years of age and because of this, Marden Lennox's will was to be read that very day. Garrick relived the past as the family gathered in the Ochre Parlor. He knew he shouldn't expect anything. In his foul disposition, something in him caused him to have the expectation that people owed him. Nothing was ever fair in his eyes for he always deserved far better than what he had received in life.

The morning sun poured through the large windows. Chairs had been positioned to face the family's attorney, who sat in the center.

"Garrick, won't you please have a seat here with us?" Elmira, his mother, asked as she turned to look at him from where she sat. She had sandy brown hair just like Garrick. Reid on the other hand, favored his father with dark brown hair and crystal blue eyes. The difference in the half-brothers in both appearance and personality was almost staggering. Because of the vast contrast, they had never been close.

Reid, who sat beside her, also glanced at him. Garrick had purposely distanced himself. Instead of joining his family and Saerlaith's two stewards, he leaned against the white marble column at the entrance to the parlor.

"This has to do with all of us," Elmira urged.

"I'm fine," he gruffly replied and was glad she didn't push it further. *Why should I? This certainly doesn't have anything to do with me. I'd be better off not being here at all,* Garrick told himself, however, nothing would have swayed him in coming. He might not receive anything from Marden's will, but he definitely wished to know just how much the marquess had given to his beloved son, Reid.

"I, Marden Lennox, The Most Honourable Marquess of Cantrell bequeth to Reid Lennox, The Most Honourable Marquess of Kerrich," the attorny began. Garrick could care less about the legal process that droned on. He toned out most of what the attorny said and merely waited to hear of Reid's inheritance and maybe the mentioning of his own name.

Sure enough, Garrick received nothing. He glared over at his half brother, Reid.

Look at him. Just sitting there all calm as if nothing out of the ordinary has happened. It's all an act to get to me! Will I ever be free from him...always lording everything over me? Well, no more! The smug look on Reid's face was Garrick's undoing.

"Garrick!" Elmira called after him when he stomped out of the room.

"Garrick, come back," Reid put in.

"No. I don't want any of it anyway," he shouted back from the hall then slammed the door behind him. *I'm sure Reid wants nothing more than for me to stay and hear just how rich he has become. Well, I won't be bossed around by him. There's no more reason to stay...it's done. What did I expect?*

"Whoa," Reid pulled the reigns until his horse came to a stop when his gaze fell upon a man sitting on a large boulder. *There he is,* he sighed. He tried to attain some compassion for his brother, yet the entire family was used to Garrick's frequent sulking. Garrick never sought to change things for in his own eyes, it was always someone else's fault for his misery.

"There you are. I've been looking everywhere for you." Reid directed his horse to approach. Garrick hadn't gone far. He never even left the land that belonged to them. It was right outside of a wooded area behind the Saerlaith. When Garrick saw him, he immediately got up and turned away from him.

"Why, so you can brag and bluster?" Just then thunder boomed and echoed over them. Reid glanced up and saw the dark clouds fast approaching. The distant waves were crashing against the rocky coast, growing louder with the coming storm.

"Certainly not. Will you just come home before this weather overtakes us?" Reid got off his horse.

"Just go away! What do you care anyway?"

"What? Of course I care," Reid slowly covered the distance between them. His keen personality, that usually commanded attention, seemed to go before him as he went. Everyone who knew Reid was drawn to the involuntary way he took charge of any situation brought to him. Garrick, on the other hand, loathed him and anyone who admired his half brother.

"You're my brother." Reid was about to put his hand on Garrick's shoulder when he pulled away.

"Don't call me that…don't pretend to be kind now. It's done! The will has been read. You can stop this act. Don't worry about me. I'll pack my things and leave."

"Don't leave Sarelaith. It's your home."

"Saerlaith has never been home to me," Garrick finally turned to face him. His dark brown eyes were filled with fury. "You know as well as I, your father could have cared less about me. He only took me in because of Mother."

"That's not true."

"Yes, I was just another charity case for him. Nothing more."

When Reid knew he wouldn't get through to him, he went on with the real reason he came after Garrick.

"Fine, think what you like. The reason I came to get you was the will."

"I see…" Garrick huffed. *He's already going to hold it over me.*

"I want to share the inheritance with you. It's not right that I should receive it all. It's more than enough for both of us." For a small second, Garrick was tempted to accept. This alone would make him rich. It wasn't long before his bitterness overtook him once more.

Reid would love for me to eagerly accept. He would surely declare it to everyone…that he alone saved me by his sacrifice. I would never hear the end of it.

Reid hoped Garrick would see reason but he was wrong. Instead of being happy at the offer, he became more livid than ever.

"I don't want your father's bloody inheritance. I don't want to share anything with you! Do you hear me?" he spewed before stomping off.

"Garrick, what can I do to change your mind? What do you want from me to sway your anger?" he yelled after him. It started to rain but Reid wouldn't give up. He went after Garrick, although he would come to regret it later.

Garrick didn't come to a stop until Reid rushed in front of him and came to a halt.

"I demand you tell me! What do you want?"

"You want to know? You really want to? Fine!" Garrick shouted. "I killed your father! I shot Marden!" His yelling held no regret or emotion. His furious confession startled Reid. It took him a moment to regain himself.

"I know that. You need not blame yourself anymore." Reid dared to put his hand on Garrick's shoulder again only to have him spitefully push it away. "It was an accident."

"To this day, you can't face the fact that Marden hated me."

"Don't say—"

"He hated me almost as much as I hated him," Garrick swiftly cut Reid off. He had struck a cord in Reid and couldn't stop now that the painful truth finally hit him. "He treated me no better than a slave...even worse than the worthless Irish."

"He did not. You know that's not true," Reid quickly defended his father. Garrick could already see the pain on Reid's face.

"Oh...and how would you know? Marden did his best to hide it in front of Mother and of course you. He would never let you...his beloved son, see his true character. You said you wanted the truth...well, this is it. I finally stood up to him when I could take no more."

"But you said it youself...that you didn't mean to and it was only an accident."

"Believe me, it was no accident." Another round of thunder was heard before the rain fell harder. Though what he said might be only partially true, the longer Garrick recalled the past, the more he was beginning to believe it to be true.

"What are you saying?" Reid beseeched, but Garrick wasn't finished with him. He finally had his brother right where he wanted him. In times past, no matter what Garrick did or said to provoke Reid, he had been unsuccessful in making him angry. Seeing the rage slowly come over him brought Garrick a kind of satisfaction he ardently sought after. It made him feel like he held something over Reid.

"Wait, what are you saying?" Anguish could be heard in Reid's voice. Garrick purposely waited before saying anything.

"Want to know something else? It never felt so good to pull that trigger and to see Marden fall to the ground."

"No... stop this," In the deluge, Reid covered his ears as if trying to push the horrible thoughts out of his mind. He was overcome with sorrow. "How could you?" he cried.

"So…you believe me at last," Garrick sighed almost happily. "Don't wish to treat me so favorably now do you…brother," his every word dripped with wicked pleasure. "Do you hate me?" Reid, who gazed at the ground, suddenly met Garrick's stare. Through the grief and heartache, Garrick saw the hatred in Reid's eyes. Garrick's efforts had finally won. He had cut Reid to the heart.

Both men nearly jumped as thunder rumbled loudly. Reid momentarily glanced up at the dark sky. When he returned his gaze on Garrick, he saw him pull out a pistol.

"Do you wish to repay me for what I've done?" Garrick asked, almost daring Reid. He held up the gun toward him. "Are you man enough to face me?" Reid's gaze was fixed on the gun before him. It beckoned to him to take it. "Go ahead." What Garrick suggested confused Reid. He couldn't figure out what was happening yet everything in him constrained him to take it. He felt like something was taking him over and he was afraid he was losing control of himself.

"Or are you too much of a coward like your bloody father?" Garrick assailed. Before he really knew what he was doing, Reid recklessly snatched the cold, wet pistol from Garrick and vehemently looked back up at him. Garrick stood, gazing back at him, willing him to go through with it. Pressure and compulsion came over Reid so greatly that he could no longer hear the hard rain or loud thunder, only the fast beating of his heart, pounding in his ears. Time seemed to slow as he raised the gun up until it was pointed right at Garrick. He looked steadily on his brother, the man who killed his father.

So much would be different if Father was still alive. Garrick stole him from me. He killed him in cold blood. All of a sudden, Reid saw what was directly behind Garrick. It was the woods. He realized for the first time that they were right outside the very woods where his father had perished. He was instantly brought back to his father's side where he held his hand tightly. He could hear Marden's labored breathing all over again.

"It's all right, son...it will be all right," Marden gasped, *"You must promise me."* Reid relived the horrible day in his mind, though he could picture it as if it had happened yesterday. He still held the gun, pointed at Garrick, but instead of seeing his brother's face, he beheld his father.

"Don't do this," Marden's words rattled Reid to his very core. Marden had never spoken those words to him that day, moments before his last breath. *"Promise me you'll continue on with my work...it's important."*

"I will," Reid promised solemnly.

"I love you, son...see you soon......"

"You will? You will what?" Garrick's question broke into Reid's unreality and brought him back to the present. It was so real to him, Reid had spoken his promise aloud. Reid felt the rain pouring over him in torrents and he caught sight of his brother again.

"What are you waiting for? Do it!" Garrick incited, "Pull the trigger!" Reid stood still. Garrick watched him closely until Reid began to lower the gun. "No! You will not back down...not this time!" Garrick took action. In his crazed state, he grabbed the pistol that was still in Reid's hand, and lifted it to his own head with a strength not his own. "End it! End it right now!" Garrick shouted. Reid could not understand what had gotten into his brother. He was mad!

"Pull it!" Garrick shouted in Reid's face. Reid tried to pull away with everything in him but it wasn't working. Though he wasn't taller than him, Garrick was stockier than Reid. He was beginning to overpower him with his added weight. "I demand you to finish this," he growled. Reid finally gave up trying to fight him and looked Garrick in the eye.

"No! I won't do this!" he boldly declared.

"You're a coward just like your father." With one last attempt, Garrick tried to anger him but it did nothing. When it was clear Reid wouldn't do it, Garrick pushed away from him and rushed into the woods.

Reid could do nothing more than stand, gazing into the trees as he began to weep. The only comfort he could find was in the promise he'd made with Marden. He eventually looked up at the dark sky. He was drenched from the hard rain but he didn't care.

"Father, I will keep my word no matter what…if it's the last thing I do."

PART
I

CHAPTER ONE

 he moment he stepped off the gangplank and onto the harbor, Reid noticed people staring at him. He was too exhausted to think much about it. The last few months had been difficult and stressful for him. All he wanted to do was go home and get reacquainted with his own bed.

He tried to ignore the stares that continued as he went over to his luggage that had just been unloaded from the ship. Reid was about to pick up a bag when a man approached.

"Please, allow me, sir." Reid glanced at him and was surprised when it wasn't one of Saerlaith's servants, but a complete stranger.

"Oh…why, thank you." Just then, he caught sight of his carriage. "Right over there please," Reid instructed the man. He then went over to pick up another piece of luggage when someone else came up to him and offered to take it for him. Reid exchanged glances with his driver, who was now helping the first man load the bag onto the carriage. He appeared to be just as bewildered by the strange act.

"Thank you again," Reid shook hands with the unknown man.

"You're the one we nade ter be thankin'," the man heartily shook Reid's hand a long while. The person beside them earnestly nodded his agreement. "Tanks for everythin' you've done for us all. I dare say, you're a hero nigh and we're proud ter have ya among us." Reid hardly knew what to say. He was taken back. He'd forgotten how news traveled, even from England. Reid had been so consumed in Parliament and keeping his father's promise, he didn't realize how people might respond. He knew and had already experienced how people felt about it in England and their resentment, yet he'd overlooked the Irish completely.

The other unknown man, wanting to show his gratitude, turned to the busy street.

"Everyone! This is Lord Reid Lennox, Marquess of Kerrich!" he shouted to the passers-by on the street. "You would chucker well ter thank this gran' paddy for because of him, we nigh have thirty Irishmen in the House of Lords! We will 'av a say in Parliament at last!" Reid was speechless as everyone within earshot immediately began to cheer and clap their praises and thanks. Even there, Reid could spot a few unhappy Englishmen among the crowd.

Everyone eventually quieted down and waited for Reid to speak.

"Thank you very much. It has been a long and hard road. I've spent my life in helping this finally come to pass. Now that it has, your kind gratitude makes it all worth it." Another round of merriment took place before Reid was on his way home. He couldn't remove the smile from his face at the thought that people had taken notice of his efforts.

The thanks from the locals continued in the following weeks and even months, afterwards. Letters came pouring into Saerlaith with an occasional spiteful note and threat. Reid was now known as the Hero of the Emerald Isle. Among the Irish, he was adored but he was also beginning to be hated by the English. His own kind despised him. All of his old acquaintances and neighboring estates acted as if they never knew the Lennox's. What hurt the most was the old friends of the family, friends of his father, who now rejected him. Through it all, Reid had kept his promise. It was what kept him going when he'd wanted to give up. During the most distressing moments while fighting for his way in Parliament, when it seemed like everyone was against him, Reid purposely made himself remember his last few precious moments with Marden. He had done what his father had fought for until the day he died.

CHAPTER TWO

March 1805

"*Y*ou couldn't have waited until we returned home?" Reid mumbled. He gently lowered his horse's leg. He was just on his way home when his horse threw a shoe. Thankfully, he was in a small village when it happened.

At least it's only a bit after lunchtime and won't be dark anytime soon.

"Come on, old boy," Reid stood up straight and led his steed to the nearest blacksmith.

It wasn't long before he was on his way again. As Reid was about to round the corner, to leave the village, he heard a familiar voice. It was Garrick.

I haven't seen him for a long while. Reid stopped walking. Ever since their encounter that stormy night, Garrick had packed up his things and left. Reid hadn't seen him since, yet he knew he wouldn't go too far since their mother, Elmira was living at Saerlaith.

Reid planned to show himself and greet his brother when he heard Garrick speaking to someone. His sudden curiosity caused him to stop and remain hidden behind a building.

"Are you now a shillelagh-hugger like your brother?" The degrading remark made Reid listen all the more intently. The next comment surprised him even more.

"Don't even put us both in the same sentence. In fact, don't mention him at all. I don't want anyone to know I'm connected to that mick. He is the laughing stock of all of England…actually wanting to help those bog-trotters." Both men snickered. Although Reid knew he shouldn't be surprised by his brother's words, it still hurt. Was this how every English landlord felt about him now?

Instead of listening to any more, Reid backed away and took a different way out of the town. However, he didn't go home straight away. He was deep in thought over what he'd overheard. He rode along the windy coast in silence for nearly an hour. This particular part of the coast rose far above the sea and became jagged and rocky cliffs. Reid could hear the large waves crashing onto the shore. The view was very pleasant indeed with the sun lowering into the water. It caused the sky to redden in color.

Just then, Reid heard another noise, though it was hard to distinguish over the wind and waves. He looked around him until his gaze fell upon someone in the distance. He finally realized it was a woman singing. Her long hair was blowing in the wind. It was reddish brown and shined in the sun. Her strong voice sounded like an angel. She was the most beautiful woman Reid had ever seen. He continued to stare at her as he slowly neared where she was walking along.

When she noticed Reid's presence, she stopped singing only for a moment and smiled at him. The act caused Reid to fall instantly in love. It was as if she had cast a spell over him with her sparkling blue eyes and full, heart shaped lips.

He couldn't take it anymore. He had to find out more about her. Reid dismounted his horse and made his way closer.

"Hello," Reid simply blurted and immediately felt like a fool. The woman finished her Gaelic song before saying a word, but he didn't mind one bit. He didn't want this to come to an end. He could listen to her forever.

"'ello," she replied and turned away from him, playing hard to get.

"Your song…your voice is beautiful. I'm Reid Lennox."

"I nu who ya are," she glanced at him frivolously.

"Oh?" Reid was drawn to her all the more by her mystery.

"You're the man who 'elped the Irish into the House of Lords. People call ya the Hero of the Emerald Isle. Reid walked around her to see her face. He was delighted when she met his gaze. He was again taken by her beauty. Her attractive features and long, free flowing hair was like none other. He knew right then and there that he wanted to make her his wife.

"And you are?"

"Eibhleann O'Breen." Even the way she said it, in her charming accent was like music to his ears. He was awestruck and completely at a loss for words. His breath caught in his throat when she boldly reached out and straightened the collar of his jacket that had folded from the wind. Her lingering touch proved that she wasn't meek in the least.

"Goodbye," she breathed and backed away very slowly. It was then that she began to sing again and drew Reid out of his dumbfounded state.

"Wait, might I see you again?"

"I'll be 'ere on the morrow," she briefly stopped, looked

back at him, and batted her eyes. Reid longingly watched her continue on her way until she was out of sight.

CHAPTER THREE

September 1805

I will not be refused today...not this time. Reid held the small ring box in his sweaty hands as he gazed out of the carriage window and watched the scenery pass by. He couldn't help but go over the last few times he'd proposed to the woman of his dreams, only to be refused every single time. The first time Eibhleann simply said no. The next two times, she had confessed that she did care for him deeply but just couldn't. The last thing Reid suspected was that she might be hiding something. Far from it. He hadn't the slightest idea of what was keeping them from getting married. He'd never known another couple in love as much as they were. They had been courting for months, spending quite a bit of time together. Reid had done everything he could think of to show his ardent love for her. He knew she returned his feelings for she showed it in nearly everything she said and did. This only added to his confusion at her refusals and the fact that she still agreed to see him right after.

Reid didn't care if she was Irish or from a poor family. All he knew was that he loved her and would do anything to make her see just how much he cared. He even purchased a larger, more expensive ring this time in hopes of proving the love he had for her.

The carriage soon came to a stop at their special meeting place. It was the very spot they'd met.

Will you marry me? I would like the honor of your hand in marriage. Please say yes, Reid rehearsed in his mind. It had to be perfect. Though, he knew very well the minute he faced her, his words would jumble up and hardly make sense. Every time he was in her presence, nothing made sense except how he felt concerning her.

He caught sight of her the moment he stepped outside. The cool wind met him but it wasn't overly cold. Eibhleann stood, gazing over the open sea. It was almost as if she was waiting for him. The breeze tugged at her skirts. Reid slowly covered the distance between them and stepped up beside her.

"'ello Reid," Eibhleann glanced up at him and greeted over the distant seagull calls. There was no point in waiting another minute. Reid anxiously pulled out the open box. The magnitude of the ring made her gasp. Reid knelt down before her, grasped her hand in his, and looked deeply into her eyes.

"Marry me?" he asked breathlessly. Eibhleann hesitated and met his hopeful gaze. Panic rose up in Reid when he detected rejection. Before she could say anything, he spoke again. "Please say yes. Please, I'll do anything…I'll be anything you want."

"I don't nu if I can, Reid," she began to pull away but Reid stood and gently took her arm.

"What is it? Are you afraid of something?"

"No…it's jist that…I've never been devoted an' dedicated to one man. I don't nu if I can be what ya want. Marriage is forever, ya nu."

"You can forget all of your doubts. I want you and you alone," he gazed at her pleadingly for some time. At least he saw a glimmer of hope in her. Eibhleann, with tears glistening in her eyes, finally glanced up at him and searched his gaze.

After what felt like an eternity to Reid, Eibhleann slowly nodded.

"Oh Eibhleann!" Reid couldn't hold back. He quickly leaned down and kissed her. "You've made me the happiest man in the world!"

CHAPTER FOUR

London, England   *June 1807*

he carriage came to a halt. Reid stepped out and helped his wife emerge. The place was very crowded for it was the entrance to the Derby. Every person of society was there in grand fashion. The couple could feel the stares and gawking as they made their way closer.

Eibhleann was endowed with jewelry, the finest clothing from France. Reid cringed at some of the hateful whispers from the crowd as they passed. He had hoped the talk and gossip over their wedding, now over a year ago, was done with. However, this was the first time he'd brought Eibhleann to London during the Season. Rumors had permeated so long that nearly every person there knew of Lord and Lady Kerrich. Rumors such as, the only reason he married her was to further his own cause in helping the Irish. That it was no more than charity. Some of the stories had made it back to Reid, yet it didn't make the whispers any easier to hear.

The tension was so great it felt almost tangible and was nipping at their heels as they walked through the gate.

The English's already poor impression of Reid Lennox had now become even worse. He'd gotten used to being called names while walking down the street, other members of parliament scoffing and laughing at him and even throwing things at him, threats, and even some vandalism at Saerlaith. But now with his wife at his side, he was beginning to fear the threatening for Eibhleann's sake.

He wanted so badly to introduce her into society and to have her experience all of the wonderful advantages of being wealthy and what the Season had to offer. He would give anything for her and had already showered her with jewels and everything she could ever want. She now looked the part of a wealthy marchioness, yet society still would not accept her or him for that matter.

"Are you alright?" Reid quietly asked and glanced at Eibhleann.

"Fine," she replied swiftly. Her uptightness told him she was rather nervous. He could see that the rude comments and snide remarks hurt her, yet through it all, she kept her head held high and remained her graceful, collected, and beautiful self. Reid suspected the same women who said those things were jealous of his wife's beauty.

Now came the worst part of finding where to sit. The hierarchy was evident as they scanned the stands.

Maybe this wasn't such a good idea to come, Reid thought.

"Lord Kerrich!" Reid turned to a man who stood and was waving at them.

"Who is that?" Eibhleann whispered.

"He is one of the new members of Parliament. An Irishman."

"Cum sit over 'ere." The man motioned to them. The seats were far from the track and a bit in the sun but they were relieved to at least be welcomed by someone.

As they made their way over, Reid became indignant.

What good is it to be wealthy? He'd asked this very question since he was only a child.

The Derby began when they sat down. Reid and Eibhleann tried their best to enjoy the race and ignore the stares.

PART II

CHAPTER FIVE

T he footman entered the townhouse and rushed up the stairs to find Reid. He was in the private sitting room just outside the bedroom. The moment Reid saw Stuart, the footman, he shot out of his chair.

"Where is the doctor?" he anxiously asked and glanced behind the footman, hoping to see the much needed doctor but there was no one.

"He wouldn't come. I went to two others but they wouldn't come either. Lady Kerrich...." Stuart was almost hesitant in his reply. "Lady Kerrich bein'...Irish and all."

"What? Why those...those bigots!" Reid fumed. He and his family had their fair share of discrimination. They had painfully found out that just because they had a great deal of money and held a title of peerage, it mattered little. They were still treated like the poor Irish they helped.

"Well, if the wealthy doctors won't help…." He didn't finish as he tried to think of what to do. Reid angrily reached up and rubbed his unshorn chin. Since Eibhleann had slipped and fallen on the front steps to their townhouse and her water had broken, things were in a whirlwind. The very last thing Reid was concerned about was his appearance and having shaved or not. Eibhleann had been in labor, with the help of a midwife, all night and it was now past lunch time the following day.

"What will we do?" he spoke aloud to himself, deep in thought as the midwife emerged from the bedroom.

"Has the doctor arrived?" she asked in a worried tone.

"No one will come," he didn't go on further for fear of the midwife also being prejudice of the Irish. Although, by her impression, it was clear she knew what was going on.

"What? She needs a doctor! Something is wrong…it has been too long. She requires a doctor's skill," she wrung her hands together.

"What can we do?" Reid asked.

"My husband! He's a doctor. Not a fancy one mind you…as you're probably accustom to, but he'll help anyone regardless of stature."

For this reason alone is surely why he isn't well known, Reid thought. "Yes! Anything," he instantly replied.

Reid was sitting stiffly near the stone fireplace when the footman led the doctor into the room. The man looked at him in all seriousness and removed his black cloak. He wasn't much older than Reid, but he looked worn with stress as if he held much on his shoulders. Reid could see some grey hair on him as well after he removed his hat. Reid was about to stand just as the midwife opened the door.

"Thank goodness you're here!" she breathed. The doctor silently rushed into the bedroom and swiftly shut the door behind him. Reid was left alone once again. He remained seated, staring at the door to the room, barely blinking. He didn't leave the spot until he heard Eibhleann cry out in pain. Reid jumped to his feet. He couldn't bear hearing her suffer through labor and not being able to help her somehow.

Reid had just wandered over to the window when he heard the door open. He turned to see it was the doctor. The worried look on his face caused fear to wash over Reid. He took a step toward the doctor but couldn't make himself ask what was wrong.

"Your wife is doing fine, just very weary," the doctor took initiative and solemnly stated.

"But what?" Reid forced himself to ask in a whisper. The man sighed heavily before replying.

"If only I could have gotten here sooner. I'm—" Reid didn't wait for him to finish and rushed into the bedroom. His eyes instantly went to Eibhleann. She lay on the canopy bed with her head to the side, quietly weeping against the pillow. Reid's gaze then moved to a small, lifeless bundle atop the nearby dresser as he began to openly cry as well. He walked in further and carefully sat on the edge of the bed to be near Eibhleann. However, once there, she turned away from him and so she wouldn't have to look him in the eye. Reid knew she was heartbroken. He was also. His only comfort was that Eibhleann was still alive and well. All he could do was take her hand.

The only thing that was certain in his mind was the hate he felt towards the rich doctors. His child was dead because of their discrimination. It was then another thought came to Reid.

"What was the gender?" he quietly asked, his voice wavered with emotion. He immediately regretted his question when Eibhleann began to sob louder.

"She refused to be told," the midwife replied. She too had tears brimming in her eyes as she was cleaning things up.

"What's to become of...." Reid began. The doctor, who was gathering his things and putting them back in his black bag, met his gaze.

"We will take care of it," he quietly replied and clasped his bag shut.

Reid returned his gaze to Eibhleann and continued to hold her hand as the midwife and doctor took their leave.

"I can't help but feel for the poor dears to have to suffer such a tragedy," Mrs. Blakeslee sighed heavily on their ride home in their humble buggy.

"Aye. Things happen though. Lady Kerrich is healthy. They'll have more," Doctor Blakeslee said. A hint of sadness could be heard in his words as well as seen on his face.

"It's a shame you couldn't have been fetched sooner," she went on.

They both grew silent as they rounded the corner and entered the east side, the much poorer part of London.

"What is it?" her husband asked when Mrs. Blakeslee abruptly glanced behind them.

"I thought I heard something like a…oh, it's nothing," she turned back to the front when she suddenly gasped, "Stanford! It couldn't be!"

"What's gotten in to you?"

"Stop the buggy!" she placed her hand on his arm as he pulled the reigns. The very moment they came to a halt, she quickly climbed out and hastened to the back of the buggy.

"Merrill, stop this nonsense."

"Stanford, come quick!" her troubled tone of voice made him act. He rushed to his wife's side to find her holding the bundle. Was his eyes playing tricks on him or was it moving?

"It's a miracle! The babe is alive!" Merrill cried.

"Just barely," Stanford began to check its vital signs. "This might be astonishing but it doesn't mean it will live." He didn't want to give his wife false hope. She met his gaze but didn't say anything. Instead, she began to cry as she nuzzled the tiny infant.

"Stanford, we've prayed for so long."

"What exactly are you suggesting?"

"You said yourself that the dear thing might not live. It would only break the lord and lady's heart more if we returned their child, only for it not to make it. We've prayed for so long for our own. Might this be God at work?" she sniffed. Stanford only sighed.

"Do you realize what this would mean?" he tried not to toy with the idea. He truly wanted a son or daughter as much as his wife.

"This infant is a sign from above. I'm sure of it. It surely needs very special care that only you can provide. What better way than to have it under our very roof?" Merrill went on.

"But—"

"Who will if we don't? The other doctors refused to come. If you don't, who will?"

CHAPTER SIX

Saerlaith, Ireland   *August 1815*

 elcome home, My Lord and Lady," the butler
greeted as he opened the door and Reid and
Eibhleann came inside. A footman took Eibhleann's
cloak before she walked through the Great Hall and
to the stairs.

"Are you going to rest?"

"Yes," was all she said before ascending. Elmira was just
coming down to see them when she met her daughter-in-law on
the stairs.

"Welcome home, dear."

"'ello."

"Are you feeling any better?"

"Some." Eibhleann's monotone, unfeeling reply clearly
showed how she was truly doing.

"Hello, Mother. How are you?" Reid glanced up at Elmira as she finished descending the stairs.

"Just fine." Her reply was always the same. She would never allow herself to reveal her true feelings. Elmira was strong and always held herself gracefully but Reid wasn't fooled. There was sadness in her voice ever since Marden died. However, even before that, Elmira had never been the most open person. Her relationship with her own two sons had never gone further than the surface.

"I passed Eibhleann. How is she doing?" Elmira asked.

"Still depressed. I had hoped the Season would brighten her spirits but it did little. The loss weighs heavily on her."

"She just needs some time, I suppose. All will be fine," Elmira patted his arm.

"Good morning," Reid spoke when his wife entered the bright dining room. He instantly thought she looked better. Her hair was fixed nicely along with her dressier attire.

"Mornin'," Eibhleann sat down at the long mahogany table and sighed heavily as if bored.

"Did you sleep well?"

"Aye."

Reid continued to watch her closely when breakfast was served and they began to eat. He thought she seemed alright. The only thing out of the ordinary was she barely ate and only pushed the food around on her plate.

Reid was nearly finished when Eibhleann glanced up at him.
"I think I'll go visit me parents today."

"That sounds like a good idea. I have one thing to get done in the study then I'll be ready to accompany—"

"I'd loike to go alone, thank you," Eibhleann cut in and gazed back down at her plate.

"Oh...a...alright. Are you sure you're feeling up to going alone?"

"Aye. I'll 'ardly be alone with the driver." Her curt reply caused Reid to feel rising tension between them. He knew he'd gone too far. Eibhleann was very free spirited and did what she liked. If she ever thought she must ask for permission about anything she would go ahead and do the very thing to the extreme, in her rebellion. However, she'd always been this way and it was one of the things Reid had fallen in love with. Her passion and proud independence was something he could never wish to have. He was and had always been a dutiful, responsible son, always doing the right thing and trying to please others. His father expected him to continue on with his work, and he had. Because of this, being rejected by society and family friends was extremely hard for him. Reid didn't like being disliked by anyone. If not for the adoration from the Irish, he might have given up.

Reid's suspicions that Eibhleann was angry at him was confirmed when she said nothing for the remainder of the meal. Once she finished eating, she merely got up and left the room.

"My Lord," Roland Carver knocked on the open door to Reid's study. Reid looked up from his desk.

"Mr. Carver, please come in," he sat back in his chair as the steward approached.

"I've just come from the McCarthy's place. They're having a difficult time with their south field. Their neighbor assumes that part of McCarthy's land belongs to him."

"Is that so? George Healy owns the land beside them, am I right?" Reid asked.

"Aye," Roland replied.

"Well, I've only known him to be peaceful. Perhaps I'll pay him a visit myself." Just then, Reid looked past his steward and caught sight of Eibhleann, who walked passed his study. "Please excuse me for a moment," he quickly stood and went after her.

"Eibhleann," he called down the hall. When she stopped she hesitantly turned to meet his gaze as if guilty of something. "Where are you going?" Reid tried to keep his tone light so he wouldn't sound intrusive or upset at her.

"I'm goin' for a ride," she replied, exasperated as if he should have known it. With that, she went along her way. All Reid could do was watch her leave. He was helpless to do anything about it nor could he go after her without making her angry at him.

Yesterday…and now today. Is this going to become a new habit of some sort?

"Whoa," Eibhleann stopped her horse in front of the welcoming place she knew well. She took in the well-known old building. It had a small, saging porch on the front, covered in dark green vines. She glanced around the quaint village, that surrounded the place, looking for any wealthy landlords or anyone who might know her and found none. Eibhleann could breath a sigh of relief for she would find no high society here of all places. There were no prying eyes who might know her as Lady Kerrich. This was where she felt at home. She didn't realize how long it had been or how good it made her feel to be back.

Eibhleann dismounted when she heard two men, who stood on the porch. She heard them begin to holler and whistle at her the moment they saw her.

"Shane, wud ya looky 'ere. Aren't yer a finely dressed thin'!" one of the men chuckled and elbowed the other man beside him.

"Ya must be lost or I've belt me noggin' and I'm dreamin'!" Martin exclaimed. Eibhleann ignored their comments that continued as she tied her horse to a nearby post and approached the entrance. Unbeknown to the rude men, she rather liked the attention. It was something she missed.

"Is she too high and moighty to hear us 'umble folk?"

Eibhleann had just placed her hand on the door handle when one of them poked his head between her and the door. "Wud ya loike me ter show ya the way back ter wherever ya came from? Wha ye from, lovely?"

"Wouldn't you two micks loike to know," Eibhleann smiled sweetly in her coy way before pushing the stunned man out of her way and walking inside. The moment they heard her Irish accent, the two men recognised her.

"Golly! Martin, wud ya believe it's Eibhleann!" he called to his friend and grinned.

"She's back?" the men gasped then they both hurried inside after her.

"Eibhleann's back!" he loudly announced to everyone once inside. It was followed by loud cheers by the locals. The bar was packed with people sitting around it and also at the several tables in the midsize room. Eibhleann inhaled deeply and took in the familiar smells. The sweet smell of pipe tobacco, the hint of stale ale from years of merriment was mixed with aroma of baking bread and rough hewn wood. It filled the air. She eventually exhaled in satisfaction as she realized just how wonderful it felt to be back.

"Kari, brin' our long lost lass 'ere some ale," Shane shouted to the barmaid. Eibhleann was instantly surrounded by old friends and assailed with questions.

"Where have ya been?"

"How's life nigh that you're rich an' too grand for the likes of us now?" Eibhleann loved it. The kind of attention she received here was all she wanted.

"It has it's good an' bad times. It's been so long since me last visit," she answered them.

The two men Eibhleann had first encountered came up beside her. One of which casually put his arm around her.

"I knew it wus you straight away."

"Ha!" Eibhleann laughed.

"Well…maybe. Anyway, nigh that you're 'ere, will ya let your hair down an' sing for us?" Shane hopefully asked. A round of cheers broke out again and didn't stop until Eibhleann whole heartedly gave in.

CHAPTER SEVEN

eid tapped his fingers on the table, growing more impatient as each minute passed.

"Dear, I'm sure there's a suitable explanation for her absence," Elmira tried to encourage him but it did little to cheer him up. "Perhaps you should have a footman go out and look for her. Her horse could have come up lame or something."

"She's been gone every day now…each time she returns later. I won't put up with—" Reid's ranting instantly stopped when Eibhleann wandered into the dining room. She acted as if nothing was out of the ordinary.

"'ello," she simply said. Reid's anger instantly sparked when she sat down without so much as an apology or explanation as to where she had been. Elmira glanced at Eibhleann then at her son nervously. She wondered how Eibhleann could miss the discomforting strain in the room.

"Shall we begin?" Eibhleann asked. She was just going to motion to the maid when Reid spoke.

"Before we dine, might I ask what was keeping you? We were beginning to worry." Eibhleann looked at him with an innocence that caused guilt to rise in him at his somberness and accusing way.

"I was at me parents t'be sure and lost track of time," she momentarily glanced at Elmira and saw she had gained her compassion.

Reid now didn't know what to say. His anger held no ground any longer.

"Am I not allowed ter visit them?" her innocent guise subsided and her tone was now merciless.

"It's not that…it just seems like it's getting later and later. You've been gone every day since we've returned from London. First you were home at teatime, then later in the afternoon…now late for dinner."

"Well, I see I must announce ter the world of my whereabouts an' me every moment. I didn't nu I 'ad to tell ya every minute of my schedule!" Reid saw that he had gone too far yet again. Eibhleann stood up quickly and threw her napkin down on the table.

"Eibhleann, don't go. I'm sorry," Reid spoke.

"Do you nu how difficult it has been for me these few months?" her voice wavered with emotion on her way out of the room.

"I'm sorry for overreacting," he tried again.

"I'll dine in me room." Reid and Elmira heard her speak to the staff.

Now I've done it, he sighed miserably.

Reid didn't feel any better the next evening. Eibhleann didn't eat breakfast or lunch with him. Reid finally asked her ladies maid if she had seen her and where she was. All the maid could tell him was that she'd gone to see her parents very early.

All day he had to fight the urge to also pay his wife's parents a visit, yet he didn't want to interefere. He didn't want to make her more upset at him than she already was. However, as the sun went down and it started to get dark, Reid's frustration rose all over again.

She's never been this late! What could she possibly be doing there all day? This is becoming ridiculous. Reid angrily paced back and forth in his room. He just so happened to go to the window and leaned against the sill. As if on cue, he spotted Eibhleann coming out of the stable and to the house. He quickly moved away from the window and behind the heavy plum draperies to remain unseen. He still watched her intently. She strolled toward the servant's entrance at a leisurely pace. The first thing he noticed was her beautiful, long hair was down. It covered her shoulders and fell below her waist.

What is going on here? Reid asked himself as he watched her stop just outside the door and pinned her hair up. Once Eibhleann had secured her dark hair in an upswept motion, she appeared to take a deep breath and opened the side door. Before walking inside however, she hesitated for a moment. She turned to glance behind her then finally slipped inside. Reid was now more confused then ever.

CHAPTER EIGHT

The couple remained silent as the open carriage rode through a village. The sun was shining and the birds singing. Reid hardly noticed the lovely day, nor did he find much joy in it. His situation weighed heavily on him.

When did going to a luncheon become so ill at ease? Reid thought when he quickly glanced over at his wife, who was looking the other way. He had hoped the small dinner party would brighten Eibhleann's spirits a bit. It was a rare occasion to be invited to anything anymore, much less a fellow English member of peerage. Reid had instantly accepted the invitation in utter surprise. However, now he wondered if it was a mistake. Things at Saerlaith were anything but normal as of late and the awkward tension was growing between the husband and wife.

Reid couldn't help but remember a time not very long ago when they would be talking almost nonstop on their way to various places. Then, it was all new to Eibhleann. When they married, she had literally started a new life. She was no longer a maid, working hard at another estate. Everything she had ever dreamed of having, was now hers. Fancy ball gowns, servants, the Season, jewels, people waiting on her and calling her Lady Kerrich, was now at her disposal. The only thing left granted her was the approval of high society. At first it had bothered them both, yet Eibhleann had never known any different. Her entire life had been surrounded by cruelty and discrimination.

As the carriage rounded the corner, they entered a less than honorable place in the village. They still hadn't spoken a word to one another, that is until the unthinkable happened. A middle-aged man emerged from one of the buildings. By the way he walked it appeared that he was loaded with spirits. *Most likely the effect of a night filled with nonsense,* Reid thought. The man was about to cross the street but waited for their carriage to pass. As they did, the man gazed at Eibhleann as if he knew her and waved perhaps a bit too friendly. Questions immediately flashed through Reid's mind. Eibhleann turned to him and found him already gazing at her. She looked nervous. Reid couldn't hold back any longer.

"Who was that?" Before he could stop himself, Reid blurted the question.

"I don't nu," she replied, sounding incredulous at his absurd question.

"Well it certainly looks like he knows you."

"That is preposterous!" she exclaimed before they both fell silent.

A few more minutes had passed before the large white estate came into view. Each of them struggled with their own thoughts until they arrived and the carriage came to a halt in front of the entrance.

"You forget I used to live not far from that village, growin' up." Eibhleann took ahold of the skirt of her bright day dress and stood up. She obviously wasn't going to wait for Reid to help her step out of the carriage. Her reason did nothing to ease Reid's mind.

Perhaps she speaks the truth...yet who could recognize her in her fine attire and fancy carriage? he asked himself but this time kept his thoughts to himself.

"I'm sorry but I'm going to have to dismiss you. I can't employ staff who can't be trusted," Reid finished and nodded to his footman, instructing him to escourt the crying young maid out to gather her belongings.

Reid felt awful to have to fire the seemingly sweet girl. He turned to Eibhleann, who sat against the edge of his desk and sighed.

"It 'ad to be done," she simply said.

"I know but it's difficult for me. She was the very last person I would assume might steal from us."

"Sometimes the people who appear loike that are the very ones," Eibhleann stood. She was evidently tired of discussing it further and just wanted to move on. "Don't tink on it any further. She'll fend somewhere else ter work." She moved passed the bookshelves and to the door, unfeeling.

"Still...it doesn't make any sense. What if I was wrong to accuse her?" Reid asked. Eibhleann suddenly stopped.

"Are ya sayin' I was mistaken? That I'm the one who's

lyin'?" she turned to face him.

"No, no. You know I'm not. It just doesn't add up, that's all."

"Well, the way I clap it, you wud take that maid's ward over mine...your wife!"

"No...." Reid covered the distance between them and took her hand in his. "I didn't mean it like that." He didn't want to fight anymore. He didn't want any more animosity between them so he decided to try to make things right on his part.

Reid was surprised when Eibhleann allowed him to kiss her.

"I'm sorry," he breathed. Eibhleann gave a quick nod then went to the door. When her face was hidden from sight, she smiled cunningly to herself. She still had Reid wrapped around her finger.

CHAPTER NINE

September 1815

The weather seemed fair enough upon first setting out from Saerlaith on the brisk fall day. It soon turned out to be quite windy and the open fields provided no shelter for his five mile ride. Reid pulled the collar of his jacket against his face to shield it as the small shanty came into view.

Reid got off his horse, walked up to the door, and knocked. He could hear the floor creak inside with someone coming to the door. The moment the man of the house opened it, he gasped.

"Oh, Me Lord! Ter what do I owe this 'onor? Please cum in, cum in!" Sean McCarthy opened the door for him to enter. All the Irish revered him the same. So much so, Reid felt like a king among them. The room was quaint yet cozy and the fireplace was warm.

"I just wanted to pay a visit and see how it is going with you," Reid answered. After he shooed his several children away from the small table, McCarthy offered him the best seat as his wife got him something to eat and drink. They had so little, yet they kindly offered what they did have.

McCarthy was a short, humble man. His ardent efforts to make sure his family was taken care of could be seen on his person. His tired face, thick build, and large rough hands proved that he wasn't afraid of work.

"Has there been any more trouble with Mr. Healy?"

"Naw, surely not after yisser steward, Mr. Carver set 'im straight. As a matter av fact, we drank together at the pub jist last noight."

"Good, I'm glad to hear it," Reid replied. They spoke about the weather and the current harvest while Reid sipped the coffee brought to him.

"Well, I don't want to impose on your family any longer," Reid stood when he'd finished and had warmed himself enough for the return journey home. "I only wanted to make sure everything was going smoothly now."

"Me Lord, you av all people cud never impose. You're a Godsend ter us all an' are alwus most failte here," McCarthy walked Reid outside.

"Uh, before ya go, 'ave ya 'eard of the blather lately?"

"No…does it have to do with the Irish in parliament?" Reid asked. Both men stopped just outside the door.

"Not exactly."

"Oh, I know…the scandal about my wife being Irish."

"Well, somethin' loike that, but…." McCarthy reasoned inside himself if he should go through with it and reveal anything about Eibhleann as Reid prepaired to walk to his horse. He then realized that if it was his own wife, he would definitely want to know.

"What do you mean?" Reid looked at McCarthy. The man's hesitant tone caused Reid to become very interested.

"I don't nu how to tell ya this."

"What is it? You can tell me."

"Yar wife...she's been seen...singin' at the pub and dancin' some." At first, Reid was completely caught off guard by this. He couldn't believe such an outrageous statement.

"It's amazing what people can come up with," Reid mumbled to himself, trying to push aside the very thought and put on his gloves. McCarthy watched him closely to see if he would believe him. The talk among the locals never stopped concerning Lady Kerrich and her present doings.

"Me Lord, I wouldn't say anythin' if I wasn't yisser friend...I uh...I've seen her there meself. I'm sorry."

All this time...she's been at a pub? "That's it then," he blurted and didn't realize he'd said it out loud. "Uh, thank you for telling me," Reid tried to compose himself but he couldn't think straight. He went to his horse and mounted it. McCarthy could sense Reid's embarrassment.

"That isn't all," he made himself continue. As painful as it was to disclose, McCarthy respected his landlord and for that reason, he had to reveal the truth.

What? What else could she possibly— Reid's mind screamed.

"She's been seen bettin' at sum horse races...or losin', I shud say. Like I said, I'm sorry, but if it were me, I wud want ter be told." By now Reid was in a daze.

"Thank you," he slowly responded. He moved his horse along but didn't look back at his tenant.

So everything she's told me has been a lie? Reid didn't know who or what to believe anymore. *Could it be true? What if McCarthy only thought he saw Eibhleann? Perhaps it wasn't her at the pub at all.* He hoped his tenant was dearly wrong. *Eibhleann wouldn't go behind my back, would she? She surely wouldn't go to a despicable place such as the common pub!* he told himself and tried to reason it away. Either way, Reid had to find out more. *Well, there's only one way to find out,* he took ahold of the reigns with purpose. He then turned his horse in the opposite direction of Saerlaith and was off.

Reid rode to where the horse races were held, yet the more he thought about Eibhleann's strange behavior of late, the more he began to doubt her innocence. By the time he reached it and dismounted, he didn't know what to think. Instead of going only by what McCarthy had told him, he wanted to find out for himself.

The track and stands of the horse races were nothing at all like the grand Derby in London. It was a bit rundown and dirty in comparison but the Irish made the most of their surroundings.

Reid walked up to the betting window.

"Place your bet, sir," the man behind the counter said, "The next race is—"

"I'm not here to place a bet," Reid solemnly interjected.

"Oh?"

"I need you to look in your records for any bets placed by Lady Kerrich."

"A...alroight," the man nervously went to a crude filing cabinet. "No one by that name is listed," he stated matter-of-factly.

"How about Eibhleann Lennox?" Reid asked and the man quickly paged through again.

"No, sir," he replied without looking up from the files.

Good! McCarthy was wrong after all, Reid breathed a sigh of relief. "Thank you for looking." He just turned to leave when he heard the man speak again.

"How about Eibhleann O'Breen?"

Reid immediately stopped and closed his eyes in dread.

So it is true. He forced himself to return to the window, not knowing if he truly wanted to know the truth or not.

"How long ago did she place her last wager?" Reid dared to ask.

"This was just last night."

"How many entries are there?"

"Quite a few in the past few weeks."

"I see. Thank you." Once he left for good, he didn't really know what his next step should be. He was hurt by his wife's rash actions and anger was slowly stirring in him. What he wanted to do was rush to find Eibhleann and blast her with questions. However, if he did it in such a manner, Reid knew well she wouldn't hear him out long enough to accomplish anything. No, he would have to go about it differently.

Perhaps I'll get a little more evidence before approaching her about it, he thought before getting back onto his horse and heading home.

When Reid returned to Saerlaith, he bounded up the front steps. Once inside the Great Hall, he quickly found Eibhleann just preparing to leave. All of his plans vanished. In seeing her, his anger roused all over again, especially when he asked where she was off to.

"I'm goin' ta me parents," Eibhleann turned to face him and her look was indignant, "Same as any other day," she sighed with irritation as she donned her cloak. Reid couldn't believe how she could blatantly lie right to his face and that he had believed her all this time. He couldn't go on like this for one more second.

"Enjoy yourself at the pub tonight." Eibhleann was going for the door when Reid spoke up. She froze in mid step. "Or perhaps there is a horse race or two tonight?" She was thankful her back was to her husband so he couldn't see the shocked expression on her face. His simple, straightforward statement baffled her. She didn't know what to do, much less how to respond.

Reid silently waited for her to do something. Eibhleann was swiftly gathering her thoughts before forcing herself to turn to meet his gaze.

"Excuse me?" she asked innocently.

"You know what I said," he coldly replied.

He knows? How? Does he know of everything? Eibhleann tried to come up with a response, anything to sway him.

"Is it true then?" Reid's question suddenly gave her an idea of how to escape his stern inquiring.

"Is what true?"

"You know what I speak of! The pub, horse races, not to mention stealing the money to do it. What next? Secret relations?" he raised his voice causing her to flinch. He had never shouted at her before. Eibhleann could tell that he was even a bit taken back by it. Reid however, swiftly decided to go through with his fury.

"Tell me!" he demanded.

"What are you blatherin' about? Reid, you're frightenin' me! I 'ave no idea what you're accusin' me of."

"Lies! All lies! How can I trust you're telling the truth now?" He truly wanted to believe her, yet he had sufficient proof, didn't he?

Eibhleann caught a hint of doubt in his eyes, giving her a glimmer of hope. She swiftly changed her demeanor. She slowly approached, reached up, and lovingly touched Reid's face. He didn't move a muscle but just continued to glare at her.

"I love ya. Can't you see I'm tryin'? Can't ya clap I'm 'avin' a rough time?" Eibhleann made her voice waver. What she said was somewhat true.

"Someone saw you there…at the pub, and I have—" Reid began in an uncaring tone but stopped when Eibhleann instantly backed away, her eyes filled with tears.

"You're 'avin' people spy on me? Ya really don't trust me. How cud ya?" Reid was now confused. He was the one who should be angry, not Eibhleann. Yet, was this another lie?

"Wait, that's not the point."

"I thought ya loved me! I thought what we shared was somethin' special. If ya love someone, you trust them! And nigh I cum ter find out you think I'm goin' behind your back al' this time?" she began to rant.

"Wait a minute!" Reid shouted to try and interpose but Eibhleann only continued.

"Why did you ever marry me if al' ya think I am is a liar?" Now it was her turn to yell. She then started for the door in a hurry.

"You're not leaving yet," Reid quickly went after her and grabbed her arm. Eibhleann feared that he had seen through her charade. But she couldn't back down now. She defiantly looked up at him, tears streaming down her face. "We need to talk about this," he insisted.

"Naw, not when there's no trust between us. Did ya ever think whoever towl yer these preposterous things might be mistaken? Or perhaps they're the ones who are lyin'!" Eibhleann ripped her arm from his grasp and left.

Reid felt like a fool.

She finally speaks the truth, he sighed in frustration, *There is no trust between us any longer.*

"Ya wanted ter see me?"

"Yes, I need something taken care of."

"I'm listenin'."

"You know of Lord Kerrich well." The man nodded. "And you also know how most of Ireland feels about him...well, everyone but the Irish idiots themselves." The man scoffed at this, causing the other to reconsider his words. "Not you of course. I suppose there are a few exceptions."

"Aye, ya headin' to tell me or not?" he asked impatiently.

"It would only be agreeable to everyone to have him and his preposterous ideas out of the way...for good."

"How shud I chucker it?"

"I don't care. Do it any way you like," he answered heartlessly. "But I don't want any part of it...no connection. Understand?"

"Aye."

CHAPTER TEN

Eibhleann finished her song and curtsied. It was immediately followed by clapping and cheering. She could feel one man's intent gaze. He'd been watching her all evening and clapping the loudest after each of her songs. She had played hard to get all night but now that things were winding down and the pub about to close, she wanted to find out more about the mysterious and handsome man that appeared to be enamored with her.

Everyone in the pub begged her to sing another, but she turned them down. However, she managed to meet the certain man's gaze and smiled flirtatiously. Eibhleann made her way to where her things were at a table. She knew he still followed her with his piercing dark eyes. He sat at a table in the corner alone. She guessed that he might come over to her at any moment.

"Splendid job, love," an old man congratulated her.

"Thank ya. Say, do ya know the paddy over there?" Eibhleann glanced in the man's direction and sure enough, his gaze was still fixed on her. He looked a bit gruff and maybe a little rough around the edges yet there was a ruggedness and errant way about him. It called out to her own willful disposition. He was robust, with black hair, and the beginnings of a beard. His unrelenting stare stood out to her. It showed a determination in him that could not be swayed.

"Why sure. That's John McNeil."

"Does he 'av business in town or somethin'?"

"Don't nu, other than that he is a captain," he replied.

"A captain, huh? Hmm," Eibhleann smiled to herself. Just as she had guessed, the very man approached at that moment.

"Have ya 'eard anymore between the lord and lady?"

"Not lately. Not since their loud quarrel some weeks ago." The two maids went about their duties, dusting and picking up in the study.

"I feel for the couple."

"Have they alwus been at odds with each other?" the younger of the two asked. She was fairly new to Saerlaith. She was hired to replace the other maid, who was fired for stealing.

"Oh naw, there used ter be such love in this house. Lady Kerrich wud sing nearly al' the time. She has an amazin' voice."

"Do ya think all we've heard is true?"

"Don't nu for certain. There's been such blather about her

bein' seen singin' at pubs and somethin' about horse races. Yet, nothin' can hold a candle to the newest talk of late."

"And what is that?"

"Well, I shouldn't be sayin' dis."

"Oh please? I won't tell a soul." The older maid hesitated until she couldn't keep it to herself any longer.

"People say Lady Kerrich is keepin' company with a certain captain these days. They say they spend almost every day together."

"Oh my," the other woman gasped.

"It's a shame t'be sure," she clicked her tongue and was about to dust the shelf behind the door when it suddenly opened by none other than Reid. Both ladies gasped and hoped he hadn't overheard their gossip.

"My Lord," they both gave a quick curtsy and started to leave, for it was customary for the staff to take care of the house without being seen or heard by the family who lived there. Before they could escape completely, Reid spoke.

"Please, don't go just yet." Both women instantly stiffened. They knew all too well they were in danger of being fired on the spot with such talk about the lady of the house. They nervously shuffled back inside the study.

"My Lord, please I…we didn't…." the younger woman made matters worse by trying to explain herself. Only the other woman knew a maid never spoke to the lord and lady unless addressed.

"You don't need to fear," Reid assured, "I did indeed hear some of what you said, but could you tell me where you heard this from and when?" The maids looked at each other anxiously. "Don't be afraid. You're job here is quite secure." With a little more urging, the older woman apprehensively told Reid what he wanted to hear.

"It wasn't any particular person, My Lord. Just sum mindless rumors on me way ter the market the other day." Before speaking, Reid pondered over what she'd said.

"You may go," he finally sighed.

"Yes, My Lord," both women breathed barely over a whisper and scurried away.

Reid watched them leave then plopped down in the nearest chair. He rubbed his face in his hands in frustration. His worst fear had come to past.

How could she do this to me? Right after accusing me of wrongly judging her...of not trusting her. And now she's with another man. Reid was so angry he could hardly contain himself. The worst part was knowing his wife was probably with the so called captain at that very moment. *Wait until she comes home and I confront her once and for all. This time I will not be swayed.*

Eibhleann made her way down the hall and to the bedroom. She carefully opened the door and tiptoed in so not to wake Reid. She was about to cross the dimly lit room to her dressing room when someone spoke and caused her to jump in surprise.

"I see you're finally home."

"Oh!" Eibhleann gasped and saw that Reid wasn't in bed at all, but sitting in a chair beside the fireplace, facing the bed. "What are ya doin' up?"

"Waiting for you," he replied in a cold tone of voice.

"Me parents begged me ter stay late." Reid was in no mood for her games. Ever since learning the truth earlier that evening, he'd furiously paced and thought of all the things he would say once his wife returned home.

"We need to talk," he lit the candle on the side table next to him.

"Can't it wait 'til mornin'? I'm much too tired tonight."

"I know." The crass statement made Eibhleann meet his gaze. "I know all about you and your captain." Reid waited to see if she would finally confess to the reoccurring accusations said of her.

"What are you blatherin' about nigh?" To his dismay, she did the same thing she always did. Eibhleann denied it and put on her feigned innocence. Little did she know, he would have none of it this time.

"That's enough!" Reid shot to his feet and marched up to her, "You will not treat me as the fool any longer. We both know…everyone knows! You will tell me the truth and you will tell me now!" He knew his demanding tone was more than loathsome to her but he didn't care. He had nothing to lose anymore, or so he thought.

"I will not be spoken ter this way!" Eibhleann spewed and was about to flee like always. However, Reid quickly caught her wrist then moved between her and the door. The moment he pulled her to him, she angrily glared up at him. Since there was no use avoiding him anymore, she would meet his fury head on with her own.

"You knew what I wus loike before ya married me! Ya knew I wouldn't be trained or broken loike sum wild animal. An' I surely wouldn't be submissive to yer. You knew who you were getting!" she spitefully spoke only inches from his face in defiance. He had no attachment or hold over her.

"So did you! I've given you everything," Reid's voice softened which made Eibhleann even madder. "I saved you from the horrible conditions you were accustomed to…practically starving. You have no want! I've provided everything. What do you want from me?" he asked, exasperated. Eibhleann pulled away from his grasp yet stood her ground instead of trying to escape.

"He adores me," she folded her arms and mumbled something under her breath.

"What was that?" he asked. Eibhleann wasn't finished being malicious. She wanted to thoroughly hurt Reid.

"John McNeil adores me an' hangs on me every word. He lets me be who I truly am. He wud do anythin' for me." The way she spoke of this perfect stranger hit Reid hard. She was relentless. "He's the kind av man yer cud never 'ope to be!" she shouted.

Reid couldn't stand it anymore. His temper had reached its limit.

"I'll have no more of your disrespect. No more!" Before he knew what he was doing, he stepped up to Eibhleann, raised his hand, and struck her. She shrieked by his abrupt action then glanced up at him. She placed her hand on her face with tears brimming in her eyes. Nothing more was said between them as Eibhleann rushed out of the room.

CHAPTER ELEVEN

*R*eid entered the dining room and found his mother already eating breakfast at the far end of the long table. She was all alone.

No sign of Eibhleann, he thought but wasn't surprised. Reid carelessly sat down in the chair across from Elmira and covered his mouth as he yawned. He was so exhausted from the sleepless night he'd endured. Part of him earnestly regretted his rash actions, yet he was still very angry at his wife.

He was about to speak to his mother when a footman, holding a tray, approached. "Your mail, My Lord."

"Thank you. Do you know where Eibhleann is? Is she here somewhere?" Reid asked and tried to ignore his mother's concerned stare.

"She left the grounds last night and hasn't returned yet."

Reid figured as much, yet he feared Eibhleann might never come home again after he'd lost his temper.

"Please let me know the minute she does."

"Yes, My Lord."

Elmira didn't say anything until the footman left.

"Are there still problems between the two of you?" she asked as if she didn't already know. Everyone at Saerlaith was affected by the growing stress and tension. Reid knew she was bound to ask sooner or later, yet he didn't know quite how to respond.

"Well...yes. I believe it's slowly getting worse." Reid felt like a failure, not only in his marriage, but losing his temper the night before.

Eibhleann didn't return until that evening. Reid was informed straight away and he stopped what he was doing. Although he realized he wasn't the only one to blame, he knew he must speak with her, or at least try.

Reid left his study and went to their bedroom where the staff said she was. When he entered, he found Eibhleann just coming out of her dressing room with a bag in hand. The moment she saw him, Eibhleann stiffened and looked like all she wanted to do was bolt for the door. Reid also was taken aback by seeing her, for her face was swollen and bruised where he had struck her.

Eibhleann made the first move by marching right past him, without meeting his gaze.

"Eibhleann…please," Reid pleaded and gently reached out to touch her arm, "I'm sorry."

"Don't touch me!" she shouted bitterly and quickly pushed his hand away. She then quickened her pace to escape. "Stay away!"

CHAPTER TWELVE

few days had passed and Reid had given up trying to keep tabs on Eibhleann's whereabouts. All he knew was, she was gone for days at a time, yet she would also come home for a while before going away again. However, he still hadn't seen her, for she stayed as far away from him as she possibly could, using one of the many guestrooms at Saerlaith.

The things that took up most of his time of late only added to the heaviness over him. It wasn't the kind of business he wanted to be dealing with. In the past week, strange things had been happening. Not only at Saerlaith and the land surrounding it, but with some of his tenants as well. The threats, angry riots, and vandalism had been increasing and slowly becoming more severe. As much as Reid hoped it wasn't true, he was beginning to have a sneaking suspicion that Garrick was somehow behind the hateful acts. It made him feel uneasy, not knowing where his brother was these days. Reid would much rather have him near and under close watch.

He had just come out of a small meeting with the magistrate in town. He wanted to let the authorities know of his suspicions and to see if they had any information. Unfortunately, they couldn't tell him anything. The meeting only made him feel worse. A man in his position couldn't trust anyone, for he didn't know how they even felt about him or whose side they were on. Most of them were English.

"Well, they weren't much help," Roland Carver, Reid's steward, who had accompanied him, stated and got on his horse.

"No, they weren't. Looks like we're on our own. Perhaps we should gather the tenants and our staff to have a meeting of our own. We need to begin to take some safety measures," Reid suggested.

"I agree," Roland replied.

Reid turned to his horse when he heard giggling echoing down the street. It sounded very familiar. He turned to see who it was and saw Eibhleann. She had just come out of a building, which he guessed was the pub she frequented, and was followed by a man. She was running and laughing like a young girl and was playfully chased by him. The man easily caught up with her and drew Eibhleann to himself. They were much too consumed with one another to notice Reid and his steward.

His anger rose instantly with seeing her frivolous and flirtatious manner.

Must be the captain, he grimaced. The worst part was he could do nothing about it, for Eibhleann would only avoid him at all costs. He was helpless and enraged as he ultimately mounted his horse. He had no desire whatsoever to see any more. Reid, in his embarrassment, quickly looked at Roland to see his response. Thankfully, he was looking the other way in respect. All he knew was, he couldn't take much more of this. He would lose it completely if he didn't do something about his wife and soon.

Reid's fury was not swayed by the next day. He had hoped Eibhleann would be home that morning but alas, she was not. He was painfully forced to resign himself and put off their confrontation until later. He had things to tend to elsewhere.

After lunch Reid finally gave up and left the house. He had to get some things in order with his tenants and couldn't wait at Saerlaith for his wife any longer.

He didn't return until the early evening, after conducting a meeting with a few of the head staff and tenants like he had planned.

Reid rode up to the entrance of Saerlaith in a hurry.

"Is she here?" he hopefully asked the footman the moment he approached to take the reins from him.

"Yes, My Lord."

"Please tell her to meet me in my study immediately, then make sure we are not disturbed," Reid stated in all seriousness as he dismounted and marched inside. He was going to have it out with his wife once and for all.

The butler met him at the door and held it open for him.

"My Lord," he greeted as Reid handed him his coat. "Was your meeting successful?"

"Not at all," he replied almost curtly in his hurry. Coincidentally, Eibhleann walked into the Great Hall at that very moment.

What convenient timing, he thought. The butler in turn must have overheard Reid's orders to the footman that the lord and lady were not to be disturbed because he quickly took his leave. The only other person left in the room was another footman who manned the door. He merely stood at his post and acted invisible as he was used to doing.

Eibhleann was obviously planning to leave because she was already wearing her cloak. She didn't falter at seeing her husband in the least but continued to make her way to the door. She made a point to entirely ignore Reid. She actually had the gall and expected him to move out of her way since he was partially blocking the entrance. This only made Reid's temper grow worse.

She has another thing coming if she thinks I'm going to put up with this nonsense any longer! Unbeknown to him was that Eibhleann's confidence was equal to his. She kept going until they were finally face to face. The strong animosity between them filled the room.

Eibhleann, in her frustration, opened her mouth to speak but Reid spoke first.

"Where do you think you're going?" Eibhleann only huffed in return.

"What do ya care?" she stepped to the side to go around him

and leave but Reid moved to block her. "It's none av your concern. Nigh let me pass!"

"No. I forbid it." He readily watched her cringe with anger. The thing she hated most of all was being forbidden from doing something. Reid was fully prepared and ready to face the brunt of her fury as he watched Eibhleann conjure up a reply in her enraged state. She was persuaded that he could easily be swayed as he had times before.

"Yer forbid it? Since whaen? This—"

"I will not allow you to see him anymore!" he demanded loudly. Eibhleann was again taken back by his sternness. He had never stood up to her like this before. Usually there was a hint of uncertainty in him, yet this time there was none to be found.

"You can't tell me what I can an' can't do!"

"You're my wife! I will have no more of this foolishness! And furthermore—"

"My Lord!" the footman had to interrupt loudly over their raised voices.

"What?" Being caught up in the heat of the battle, Reid shouted at him though he didn't mean to.

"I'm sorry, My Lord, but there's someone to see you. He says it's very important. Reid sighed heavily then glanced at Eibhleann, who looked as if she was up to something.

"Fine. Make sure she doesn't leave this house," he turned to the footman and pointed at his wife. Eibhleann instantly scoffed at him and started for the hall to go upstairs.

He reluctantly turned to the task at hand just as the footman opened the door and let the man inside. Reid had never laid eyes on him before. He was a middle aged man, not overly tall. He wore a wool jacket with the collar pulled up around his neck.

Who is it? He said it was important? He stepped closer nonetheless as did the stranger. It looked as if the man was going to pull his hand from his pocket to shake hands with Reid when a strange smile formed on his face. Reid couldn't figure out the almost crazed expression, yet began to extend his hand to him.

From out of nowhere, he saw that the man held something. Time seemed to slow, yet it happened very quickly so that Reid couldn't respond. He was too slow to realize the man held a pistol. His smile remained as he pointed it directly at him. Before Reid could react, the man pulled the trigger. He was so close to the gun that the blow pushed him backwards with such force, he hit the wall behind him.

Eibhleann was stomping up the stairs when the gun fired. She jumped and gasped in surprise. The loud bang was immediately followed by desperate shouts. Eibhleann spun around and flew back down to the Great Hall. The first thing her eyes were drawn to was the blood on the floor. She followed the trail of it to her gasping husband.

"Oh my!" she shrieked and ran to him.

The culprit had rushed out of the door just before Eibhleann arrived and the footman was shouting for help.

Reid couldn't breathe. He struggled for each shallow pant. He was in shock as he glanced down at his stomach. He touched the blood oozing from the large wound then looked at his hand, trying to figure out what was happening.

"Reid!" When Eibhleann came to him, he tried to take a step toward her. He only ended up falling backwards and hitting the wall again. Eibhleann tried to help him steady himself but it didn't work. Instead, he reached for her and grabbed ahold of the necklace she wore. He was too weak to stand up and began to tip. He pulled the necklace with him until it broke as he fell onto the ground.

By this time, Elmira rushed into the room along with several footmen and maids.

"Heavens! What happened?" she cried and went to her son's side.

"Someone has gone for help," one of the staff informed and, with the help of two other men, gently lifted Reid from the floor.

Eibhleann was left kneeling where her husband had lain, staring at the crimson blood on her hands.

CHAPTER THIRTEEN

T hrough the blur of unconsciousness, somewhere beyond his memory, Reid found himself in a room alone. He looked around the dim, plain room. It had no windows or doors and Reid had no recollection of it whatsoever. He tried to recall what had previously taken place but he couldn't think straight. It was as if he had no awareness of time or place. All of a sudden a single recollection struck him, though it was a bit blurry. Reid knew he had been wounded. He quickly glanced down at his stomach, yet there was no sign of any problems.

Where did it go? It's gone! He put his hands on his midsection and felt it over and over in unbelief. An awful thought was just beginning to dawn on him when the next thing he knew, the room filled with light. It was brighter than any candle or light from the sun. Reid was terrified. He felt so small, powerless, and overcome with fear, especially when he heard a voice.

"What have you done for Me?" It started as a whisper, filled with power that overtook him.

Am I hearing things? Reid asked himself for the voice could be mistaken for rushing water.

"What have you done for Me?" This time it was clearer and more resounding. Reid now realized the question was directed at him.

"I...uh...." More than anything else Reid was certain it was God. He didn't know how to respond.

"What have you done in your life for Me?" the voice persisted.

"I help people...the Irish. I've given my time and money to help them." Reid began slowly in a confused daze. His answer came out in more of a question.

"What have you done for Me?" The voice grew louder like a roaring waterfall and sounded more authoritative. Reid tried to gather his thoughts to come up with a satisfactory answer. He was swiftly growing nervous.

"I've given my life to help the Irish into Parliament to give them a voice. I've fulfilled my promise to my father." Reid recalled his deeds and was more confident this time. *There. That's certainly the answer.* Or so he thought.

"What have you done for Me?" Now Reid was becoming irritated, amazed he hadn't changed anything.

"I've done plenty! I'm an upstanding person who does the right thing." He did his best to defend himself, yet deep down he wasn't sure now. His confidence was waning.

"'There is none righteous, no, not one,'" the voice seemed to boom like thunder, causing Reid to tremble. At that very moment every sin, selfish deed, thought, word, and action flooded Reid's mind. Every single thing he'd ever done in his life flashed before him in torrents. He was now very aware of what was going on and it terrified him. Guilt and shame flooded over him and he felt as if he might be crushed, smothered by the enormity of it.

"'Though I bestow all my goods to feed the poor, and though I give my body to be burned, and have not love, it profiteth nothing.' 'for without Me ye can do nothing.'" Reid's self-confidence vanished as the voice continued and in its place was a sinking feeling in the pit of his stomach. "Your heart is far from Me. 'For if we sin wilfully after that we have received the knowledge of the truth, there remaineth no more sacrifice for sins, but a certain fearful looking for of judgement and fiery indignation...'"

An image suddenly appeared in front of Reid out of the bright light. It was as if he was looking out of a window. At first it was fuzzy. Through a haze, Reid blinked several times before he could see clearly. Reid was shaken to the very core when he saw himself. He was shirtless and horribly beaten. He was nearly unrecognizable yet he knew more than anything that he was truly beholding himself. The next thing Reid knew, he was lying on his back. He felt his arm being roughly pulled to the side, then his other arm. He glanced over and saw an unknown person place a large nail against Reid's palm. The feel of cold iron caused the hair on the back of his neck to stand on end. He shouted in pain as the nail was thrust through his hand with a sharp pounding of a hammer. One, then another, and another. Each blow was worse than the last. No matter how much he pleaded or cried out, the person was merciless as he did the same to his other hand. Reid's hands burned and pounded with unspeakable pain that resonated through his entire body, however, it wasn't over. Reid looked down, through blurred vision. His feet were placed against a piece of wood. He then shut his eyes when he caught sight of another nail. He wreathed in agony as the man finished the job of nailing him to a wooden cross. Reid felt himself being raised off the ground. Blood stung his eyes when he opened them. The distress and pain was so great he felt like he might pass out from it, but relief wouldn't come. Unseen people could be heard in the distance, scoffing and laughing at him.

"No…no!" Panic stirred in him as he found himself back in the room, watching the horror unfold. The pain he had felt on the cross remained. *This can't be! I'm too young…I'm not ready to die! I need more time!* Desperate thoughts echoed within him.

The entire room faded away into utter darkness. Reid now couldn't see a thing, not even his hand in front of his face. He had never experienced such lonely darkness. The only thing left was his tortured thoughts and quivering breath.

I have to do something…I can't just let this happen. But what? "God, I shouldn't be here! God, I didn't know. Help me!" he screamed with everything in him. He couldn't take this thick, horrible darkness anymore. He didn't know if he was just warm from his distraught state or if it was truly growing hotter as he descended. A strong smell of sulphur burned his nostrils and throat with every breath he took.

Reid had been to the high society stuffy church enough to know what was happening. The worst thing was he couldn't stop it from taking place. All of a sudden something came up in him, so small he almost missed it. It was a very faint memory of a man who had come to Saerlaith when Reid was only a boy before his father died. All he could recall was standing in the doorway as Marden spoke with the stranger. The man told them about some very different things…about Jesus. After listening to some of what he had to say, Marden treated him kindly but more or less told him he wasn't interested. Reid's father shared some food with him then sent him on his way.

Reid could picture Marden walking with the man, talking a bit more before he mounted his horse and was off.

Some of the man's peculiar statements had stayed with Reid, though he'd seldom thought of them for many years. Now that day clearly came back to him and the things the man had shared.

"Jesus said, 'I am the way, the truth, and the life: no man cometh unto the Father, but by me.' 'Whosoever believeth in him should not perish, but have everlasting life.' 'That if thou shalt confess with thy mouth the Lord Jesus, and shalt believe in thine heart that God hath raised him from the dead, thou shalt be saved.'"

That's it! "I believe!" Reid cried out, "God, I believe on Jesus! I confess Him as my Lord." He had his eyes shut tightly but it was so dark it made no difference. The haunting image came before him again. The horribly beaten man on the cross, but this time Reid didn't see himself. This time it was Jesus.

"Forgive me! I'll serve you! I make you my Lord!" In an instant, he felt as if he was going upward now and a loud whoosh, like a rushing wind, surrounded him. The moment Reid opened his eyes he felt pain in his midsection. He was on his knees in his bedroom at Saerlaith. He glanced around the large room. He was in his bedclothes and had bandages tightly wrapped around his waist. The only light came from the fireplace at the far end and the flames caused shadows to flicker on the dark walls.

Reid was still very shaken from the dream or vision. He was unable to tell how much time had passed or if what he'd gone through was real or not. Deep down, in his heart of hearts, he knew it was all too real.

I must have fallen off the bed, Reid tried to figure out what had happened. It was hard to concentrate for the pain was quickly coming back to him. Somehow he had to get back onto the bed before the affliction became too severe, causing him to pass out.

Reid reached his arm on top of the bed to try and lift himself up and groaned. He tried and tried until it became too much for him. He fell to the side and lost consciousness. It wasn't long before a maid come along to check on him.

"Oh my!" she went inside and shrieked. Reid was bleeding

through the bandages from the blow of hitting the floor.
"Someone help! He's fallen!" she ran out of the room shouting.

CHAPTER FOURTEEN

Eibhleann entered the bedroom quietly. The maid, who's turn it was to tend to Reid, saw the lady of the house. She silently got up from the chair by the bed.

"My Lady," the maid curtsied to her then slipped past her to leave. Reid was still unconscious after being discovered that he had fallen out of his bed and onto the floor. Now someone sat with him every moment.

Once she was alone in the room, Eibhleann barely glanced at her husband. She tiptoed across the room to the armour. She tried her best to remain quiet but the wood floors creaked as she went. As loud as it seemed to Eibhleann, Reid didn't stir. She had to squint in the dimly lit room to search through the various things on top of the dresser.

There it is, she sighed when she spotted the necklace. She had wondered what had become of it since the incident. Eibhleann assumed the staff found in on the floor while cleaning up the blood and might put it in their quarters. *They even cleaned it,* she picked it up and inspected the plain but meaningful gold necklace with a small pendant in the likeness of a flower. It was still broken from Reid pulling it from her neck. No matter her recent feelings toward Reid, it still held sentiment for the love they had once had for one another.

She carefully put it in her reticule then turned back to the dresser. As she browsed, Eibhleann added a few more small valuables to her handbag along the way. Though no one was in the room except her husband, she almost felt like she was being watched.

Eibhleann was ready to leave when her eyes fell upon Reid. She stopped for a moment and took in his pitiful state. His face was very pale under the dark brown whiskers that had begun to grow. He breathed loudly as if it was painful every time he inhaled. She of course felt badly about what had happened to him, yet, her thoughts of late were on something else completely. *Soon all of Saerlaith will be mine.* Her gaze was fixed on Reid and the deathly appearance. She truly had loved him once but that was all over now and had been for some time. *I'm glad I didn't leave altogether before this happened to him. He might have had time to do something drastic concerning me.* Her new plan was to stay a little closer to home for the time being to assure that things went her way.

"It will only be a matter of days for him." Eibhleann recalled the doctor's words. It had been a nasty blow, especially since the gunman had been in such close range.

Eibhleann glanced down at her purse, where she'd placed the necklace, remembering a happy memory.

Oh well, it's over now. I've found someone else to bring me happiness. She walked to the door and left, without looking back.

In the following days and weeks Reid kept hanging on but it was a very slow recovery. It was an entire month before he could leave his bed, only for minutes at a time. There was a significant amount of internal damage which was slower to heal. The doctor's main concern was infection. Reid had suffered through a severe one already, which put a stop to any healing done. He was growing much better after the fever had broken, although the doctor knew he wasn't exempt from having another.

The winter months slowly wore on and Eibhleann remained much closer to Saerlaith the entire time just in case Reid took a turn for the worst all of a sudden. Though, she never went to see him again.

The only thing that helped Reid to keep his sanity through the horribly long days, cooped up inside his quarters, was his newly found interest. It was swiftly starting to become a way of life to him. It all started in trying to recall some other things about the man who'd come to Saerlaith years ago to share the Gospel. He could still picture the man holding a Bible and reading the strange words from it. Reid quickly had someone find him one. He planned to start at the very beginning, but that was when the infection came upon him. He struggled through, yet when the doctor warned it could very well happen again, he realized he should start in the New Testament in the event that he wouldn't make it. This was where he began to read about Jesus and everything He'd done. Almost immediately, Reid realized the way he viewed God was very wrong. God wasn't a God of judgement, condemnation, and damnation as he'd thought from what he'd first experienced. Sure there were certain commandments to be upheld and it was up to you to do this, but it was much more than that. Jesus was sent to earth to show forth God's everlasting love. His sacrifice was to save them from judgement. He showed the way to be free from condemnation because He loved mankind. Jesus had given Himself as sacrifice for their sins so He might deliver them.

It was difficult for Reid to wrap his mind around Jesus' actions. He didn't quite understand how he could lay down His life for people who mocked Him and certainly didn't deserve it.

There was another thing Reid was contemplating with all his extra time. He planned to make several changes in his life and how he ran Saerlaith once he was back on his feet. The words he read from the Bible seemed to speak directly to him and he was ardently ready to carry out every one of them to the best of his ability.

January 1816

Reid had been meaning to share his experience with Eibhleann. He was waiting for the moment she would come to him but as time wore on, she never did come to see him. He could only imagine what she had been up to since he'd been shot. Reid didn't understand why she hadn't left altogether. He had asked his staff to fetch her a few times but she wouldn't oblige. He couldn't give up, not before telling her he was a changed man.

After he finished breakfast in his room, he glanced up at the maid, who was gathering his dishes.

"Could you tell Eibhleann I wish to see her?"

"Yes, My Lord."

Reid scooted against the pillows behind his back to sit up straighter, though he didn't really expect her to come. After a few moments he heard someone enter.

Probably the maid telling me she has rejected my request once again. To his surprise, Eibhleann quietly walked in. Upon seeing her for the first time in several weeks, even months, he thought her more beautiful than ever. Her hair was up with soft curls coming down onto her neck and face. The gold and emerald green dress she wore set off her eyes. It almost made her dark blue eyes appear green as well. Fond memories of their relationship, in the past few years, came flooding back to Reid. All he could do was swallow hard at the sight of her. The only encumbrance on her appearance was her anxious expression. It was as if this was the very last place she wished to be.

Reid instantly grew rather nervous for he didn't know how to even begin to explain the new change in him. He had yet to tell anyone about it, even his mother. He didn't want her to worry about him more than she already was.

Eibhleann didn't say a word but stiffly sat down in the chair beside the bed. She had to force herself to look at him and found him already gazing at her. The silence became uncomfortable quickly. It had been so long, she almost felt like a stranger to him.

Even before he had been shot, Reid's wife had grown more and more distant and the wall between them was increasing with each passing day. Reid could tell just by the look on her face that she felt the same as he did. His presence made her uneasy. Eibhlean kept waiting for him to speak and break the silence but he didn't for some time. In truth, Reid was almost afraid to speak for in times past they would only end up fighting or saying something despicable. They were unable to fight as long as they both were quiet. Eibhlean became more agitated, not knowing his motive in wanting to see her. She finally couldn't take it any longer.

"The maid said yer 'ad to speak to me." Even then, Reid didn't respond right away but mulled over how to respond.

"I didn't think you would come." There was something about him Eibhleann couldn't grasp. The look in his eye and the softness of his voice troubled her. She moved her gaze downward to her hands in her lap.

"Aye...well." Where was the anger she felt towards him? She searched within herself, trying to recall all he had done to her and how she despised him. She was unsuccessful for her confusion overpowered her thoughts.

"I've...I've been busy," she eventually blurted. Reid could feel her agony over being there. He had to get to it.

"I don't precisely know how to begin," Reid slowly went on, "First off I want to apologize."

"For what?" Eibhleann cut in and looked back up at him coldly. She immediately put up her defences against him. *What is he up to? Since when does he apologize for anything? It's surely a cover up to his true motives...perhaps to catch me in my own words.* The anger she couldn't find before sparked in full force. *He'll not get the better of me! I'm no fool,* Eibhleann thought and acted irritated as if Reid was completely wasting her time.

"For everything...for accusing you, for arguing, and above all else for striking you. You have no idea how sorry I am for my actions." Eibhleann was completely taken back when Reid actually choked with emotion.

Is this some new attempt to make me confess? Well, he is sadly mistaken! She instantly pushed aside her shock and stubbornly set her jaw and folded her arms.

Reid noticed her all too common defiant resolve. He wasn't surprised by it. He only wondered what she would do once he told her everything.

"Something happened to me when I was unconscious and it

has changed me. God spoke to me. He asked me what I had done in my life for Him and said my heart was far from Him. The only thing I had was a fearful looking to of judgement…it's difficult to explain to make you fully understand. It was more real than anything I've ever known. Eibhleann, I've made Him the Lord of my life and I plan to serve Him with all that I have and all that I am from now on," Reid stated enthusiastically and watched for her reaction. She hid her confusion well and appeared to be unimpressed.

"I don't nu what ya want me ter say to this." Reid knew better than to think her response would be any different, yet part of him hoped it nevertheless.

"I very nearly died," he went on emphatically, trying to get through to her.

"Aye, well, ya didn't." With that, Eibhleann stood.

"You sound disappointed that I'm still here," he simply said. It angered her even more.

"I jist don't understan' why you're tellin' me this. Yer situation isn't grave any longer."

"It's very important to me. It's more significant than anything else. I'm sharing this with you because it changes things…it changes everything…how I live, conduct the affairs here at Saerlaith, and us."

That's it! That is what this is all about, she thought, *He wants to start afresh and act as though nothing has happened between us at all! I will never forget.* "Us? It hasn't been aboyt us for a long scale."

"That's just it. I hasn't been but I mean to change it. I've told you all of this to show you I want to make things right in every way. You might not believe or see it right away, but I will." Reid's passion frightened her a bit. Eibhleann had seen the determined look in his eye before. She had witnessed him get his way no matter what the opposition, many times. It's what got the Irish into parliament when it seemed like everyone was against him. She didn't like this at all. What did he mean by making things right between them? What did this mean concerning her?

Like Reid, Eibhleann was also used to getting her way and presently, things were moving out of her control. Her plans were ruined! Reid was supposed to be long gone and the inheritance solely hers. And now with God being brought into it, causing this so called change of heart, it threw her even more. There was nothing more she could do. She felt the urgency to retreat. It's what she always did when things like this happened and she had no control over the situation.

"Say what ya loike but I 'av no time for this," Eibhleann huffed then did indeed leave. Reid knew all too well he couldn't say or do anything to make her stay, nor did he mean to. He had said all that was necessary for the time being. She knew the truth now and that was the first step.

CHAPTER FIFTEEN

February 1816

"*L*ord, I know it was foolish of me to think things would change quickly once I told her...but I want to make things right so badly. I want the change that's taken place in me to happen to Eibhleann as well. How do I make her see? How do I make her see I've changed? A month has passed and things are the same. God, how do I make her love me?" As silly as Reid felt for saying it, that's what it all came down to. He wanted so badly to regain Eibhleann's love. It was especially difficult for him since he was a powerful man, used to having things go his way. He desperately needed guidance but he was still very new at this.

He sat on a chair in his room near the fireplace. He stared up at the ceiling, waiting for some kind of direction. When none came, he sighed and reached over to get his Bible from the table beside him. He read along for half an hour when seemingly out of nowhere he came upon something Jesus said.

12 This is my commandment, That ye love one another, as I have loved you.

13 Greater love hath no man than this, that a man lay down his life for his friends.

"Lord, I want to do everything in my power to do what You have said. I gave You my word. I'm reading this now and I know it holds the direction I need. Please show me how...show me how to carry this out concerning Eibhleann and this situation." At that moment, Reid remembered something while reading through the other three gospels. It was the way Jesus treated Judas. It completely baffled him. Even though He knew Judas would betray Him, Jesus still loved him. He washed his feet and even went as far as to openly forgive the people who killed Him.

How could Jesus love someone who He knew would betray Him? It's unheard of! Reid kept going over this in his mind. He could maybe see dying for someone you loved and that deserved it, but people who treated you badly? It just didn't make sense. *Perhaps it's not supposed to make sense,* a thought came to him. Almost everything Jesus said and did didn't make sense to a person's mind, yet truth radiated from His words.

Reid pondered how Jesus treated Judas in comparison to the situation with his wife. She had betrayed him in several different ways.

Yet He tells us to love nevertheless, Reid mused.

"Love Eibhleann as I have loved you...regardless of what she does." There it was! It was the answer he had been diligently searching for. It sounded so simple yet so profound. Reid knew it came from outside of himself. Right then, he made a change deep

in his heart concerning her. He determined that he would lay down his life and love Eibhleann as he was loved by his Father, regardless of how she acted. No matter what she did, he wouldn't be swayed. He would fight for her love and seek to win her heart.

"Lord, I'm ready to do this. I know it starts with forgiveness. I forgive Eibhleann and choose to forget all she has done, just as You have done to me. I pray for help to carry this out and that she will grow to know You as I do. You've shown in Your word that You're love isn't dependent on us…so neither will my love be dependent on her."

March 1816

"My Lord, what a surprise to see you," Roland Carver looked up from the papers on his desk.

"I decided it was high time to get back to my duties, at least a few and very slowly, as I've promised the doctor."

"Well, I will gladly move aside," Roland got up from the desk and backed away.

"I thank you for taking care of things in my absence. I plan to just take a look at the books and see how it has been going since last fall. You can stay if you like. It won't take long for I'm confident everything has been in fine hands." Reid sat down at the desk just as Roland gathered the books for him.

The steward walked over to the large windows and gazed outside to give Reid time alone to look things over. Roland wondered what the marquess would say once he saw it. Ever since Reid was wounded, Eibhleann had taken the liberty of helping herself to a great deal. Because she was the lady of the house, no one could do or say anything about it. The books alone showed just how much she had taken over the long period of time. It bothered the steward to no end. Roland wanted nothing more than to tell Reid all about it as soon as he was well but he didn't quite know how. Some things just weren't done, especially speaking against the lady of the house.

But now I won't have to say a thing. He will see for himself.

Reid went page by page without saying a word. Roland quickly glanced at him from time to time but nothing happened. *Surely he must see the money that is unaccounted for by now.* He was amazed when Reid finally shut it and stood.

"Well, it all appears to be in order," he calmly announced. The steward went back and forth in his mind if he should say anything. He thought Reid would be furious.

Maybe if I mention something along the lines, he'll pick up on it. Before Reid could say anything more, Roland spoke. "I suppose you saw the few discrepancies in the accounts…some things that don't add up."

"Uh, yes…I did," Reid hesitated, "You kept track of it well, regardless of it." The steward was more confused than ever.

He sees it and just doesn't want to admit it or is there something else going on? Roland thought and wanted to voice his questions. *Lord Kerrich is a kind man and I've worked for him a long time. Surely it won't anger him if I say a bit more.* "Might I speak freely, My Lord?" he carefully asked.

"Of course," Reid replied without hesitation. Roland was relieved yet now to find the right words.

"After all she's done…why not dismiss her and be done with it? I dare say she's taking great advantage of her place here." There, it was finally said.

Reid was silent for a moment before a strange look formed on his face.

"It's quite the opposite of what you assume. I would do

anything for her. I would die for her." That was the very last thing Roland thought Reid would say. He was flabbergasted to say the least.

"You would die for that untrustworthy shant?" Without thinking, he frankly blurted his mind at last.

"Now you have gone too far. I will not allow you to speak of her…my wife, in such a manner," Reid's voice raised in anger.

"I'm sorry My Lord. I didn't mean to upset you." *Now what should I do?* "I…will take…my leave now," he stuttered, reached for his hat that hung on the back of the door, and left.

CHAPTER SIXTEEN

Eibhleann peeked inside Reid's study and was glad to find no one inside. She happily entered and strolled to the safe as if she hadn't a care in the world. She actually wondered how much longer she could get away with doing it this way before Reid would be back to his daily routine and duties. Then she would have to go back to how it was done before, in secret and at night.

Eibhleann was just reaching for the handle to the safe when she heard someone walk in behind her. Inside she was startled, yet she calmly reacted by nonchalantly turning around. She acted as if she owned the place because she didn't want to appear as if something was out of the ordinary. She silently breathed a sigh of relief when it was only the steward. Although it was known in the entire house what she was up to, it was a whole other matter being caught red handed by her husband. This way her actions were known but never voiced and no confrontation made. Eibhleann could care less if Roland saw what she was doing. He was below her in rank and couldn't do anything to stop her.

"My Lady, what brings you here?" he walked further in, which was odd in itself.

I don't have to answer to him! she told herself. "Ah, 'ello," she sighed. He kept coming closer.

"I come to find you here more and more often." Roland came to a halt on the other side of the desk, directly adjacent to her.

"Pardon me?" *What is he implying? Is he merely coming on to me as other men?* she asked. She was used to that sort of thing at the pub. On most occasions, she rather enjoyed the attention.

"You know what I speak of. You're not fooling anyone."

"Ya 'ave no right—" As she spoke, Roland swiftly stepped around the desk and suddenly took ahold of Eibhleann's wrist before she realized what was happening.

"Your husband might play the fool but I will not," he growled under his breath. Eibhleann was aghast yet she tried to make light of the frightening situation. The last thing she wanted to do was let him see the fear in her.

"Play the fool?" she scoffed and forced herself to chortle nervously to try and hide her alarm. "He is one! An eejit to be sure and ya 'ave no say in the matter."

"You're quite wrong about that," he smiled maliciously and tightened his grip. The act made her finally realize this was no game. She was in danger.

"Unhan' me!" she yelped from the pain in her arm, "Let me go or I'll scream!"

"You'll do no such thing," his voice lowered as he was about to pull her closer to him.

"Unhand my wife!" From out of nowhere, Reid rushed in and assailed the steward. He threw his fist into Roland's face, sending him to the floor. As soon as she was released, Eibhleann backed away. Reid wasn't finished. He grabbed Roland by the neck and pulled him to his feet.

"Don't you ever lay a finger on her again!"
"It's not what it appears, My Lord…she threw herself at me!" Roland pleaded.
"Enough! You're finished. Hughes, Gerard!" Reid shouted. The steward entreated him until the butler and footman swiftly arrived and took ahold of him. "Get him out of my house!" They heeded his orders without another word.

When the commotion was over and all grew silent, Reid glanced at Eibhleann. She was standing against the wall, holding herself and crying.
"Are you alright?" Reid stepped toward her.
"Jist leave me!" she cried. She then picked up her skirts and rushed out of the room. Reid was left alone, wondering what to do. He breathed heavily for he felt a little winded from exertion. He wasn't used to it and was still recuperating.

"I thought I might find you here." Eibhleann glanced up at Reid only to turn away and wipe her eyes.
"How?" she sniffed.
"Because," he pulled a handkerchief from his pocket and approached the large boulder Eibhleann sat upon. "This is our spot. The place we've come to all those times…to get away from the problems of the world." After handing it to her, Reid looked over the cliff and out at the beautiful coastline. It was

breathtaking every time he visited. This was the same place he'd first laid eyes on Eibhleann and proposed as well. All of the occasions hadn't been so joyous however. They had also frequented it during some of the saddest times in their life together. The last span of time had been the longest they'd ever stayed away.

Reid ached to have Eibhleann's heart again like he used to. He wanted to go to her, take her in his arms, and comfort her. Although, deep down he hoped he wasn't remembering the past wrongly.

Was her heart ever truly mine or has she been going behind my back since the beginning? he asked himself this dangerous question. It wasn't long before his convictions rose up in him. *No, I refuse to think like this any longer. I have chosen to forgive and forget and to love her unconditionally.*

"How many times do you think we've come to this spot?" Reid asked her to get his mind on something else.

"Countless," Eibhleann replied lifelessly.

"Are you alright?" he finally moved his gaze back to her. He couldn't understand her forlorn demeanor. It was almost as if she was contemplating her next move. *Why can't she see I care about her? I have no hidden motives behind my actions.*

"No, I'm not gran' so," Eibhleann exclaimed. Reid could tell wat she would say before she spoke by the way that same stubborn, defiant look came over her face.

"Did he hurt you?"

"It's not aboyt that at al'...ya jist can't grasp it, can ya?"

"Please tell me then," his calm request made her grunt in annoyance.

"If ya weren't so fond av this new unseen friend of yers, this wouldn't have ever 'appened."

What? Me? I just saved her! Reid's thoughts aroused, tempting him to snap back at her, but he gulped back his temper.

"This so called God is al' you're consumed with anymore.

There's naw room for me even if I wished it."

"God is the reason for my love for you."

"Oh, I see! If it weren't for Him, yer wud be forced to care for me alone, is that it?" she angrily stood.

"Eibhleann, can't you see I love you more than I ever have before? I know what it truly means to love you now." Reid reached out to touch her arm but she swiftly backed away. He couldn't let himself give up. The fact that she hadn't left altogether, as was the usual, gave him all the more reason to hope. Reid carefully tried again, as if he was wooing a frightened animal.

Eibhleann's arm was cold as ice at his touch and it gave him an idea. Reid took off his jacket and slowly, almost timidly stepped toward his wife. He gently placed it onto her shoulders. The simple act appeared to make an impression on her, yet Reid still couldn't figure out what she was thinking.

Without turning to face him, Eibhleann sighed before responding.

"I don't want ter share with someone who doesn't exist. It's worse nigh than ever an' I hate it! I have nathin' more to live for."

"Eibhleann, don't say such a thing."

"I mean it…an' I'm realizin' jist how true so 'tis more and more," Eibhleann glanced at him with bitter tears in her eyes, filled with rejection. She pushed his jacket to the ground before stomping away.

CHAPTER SEVENTEEN

eid sat down at his desk, ready to meet the day, head on. He had been back to his normal routine for a full week now with no ill effects. Usually if he overdid it in the least, he would pay for it the following few days with weakness and pain. So far, the past few days had gone very well. It had never felt so good to be back to his tasks.

He took in the small pile of papers on top of his desk when something out of the ordinary caught his eye. It was an envelope with his first name written on it.

It's in Eibhleann's handwriting! Reid couldn't help but smile. He had been praying hard for her lately. *Perhaps it's finally paying off and she's coming around.* He hadn't seen her since their meeting on the coast a little over a week ago, though he'd been informed that she had been at Saerlaith somewhat.

Reid excitedly opened the envelope and pulled out the note.

Reid,

I've thought long and hard about what you said at our place and I've realized something. You are indeed a different person then before being injured...

Reid's breath caught in his throat.

Is this a dream come true? Is Eibhleann coming to the Truth at long last? he hoped as he hurried to read the rest of the note.

The person you are now is someone I can never grasp or understand and I can't bear it any longer. I'm not good enough, nor will I ever be, to meet your high expectations. You've seen the truth and are perfect in your own sight. I can never be good enough.

I truly meant what I said. I have nothing more to live for. I don't want to go on living anymore. Not like this. I've tried to find a way but can't. It's really for the best. The only way for you to find happiness is when I'm gone.

I did love you once. Remember the good times we shared.

Farewell,

Eibhleann

Reid instantly shot out of his chair, dazed. Thousands of thoughts flashed through his mind as tears flooded his vision.

"No, she can't do this!" he choked as his mind raced with questions of what to do. Out of his emotions and reeling thoughts came one thing. *Go!*

He dropped the note to the floor and dashed out of his study. Reid raced down the steps, willing his feet to move faster, to the nearest door. Just outside, a footman was climbing onto a horse when Reid came up, grabbed him from behind, and pulled him down from the saddle.

"My Lord, is everthin' all right?" the bewildered footman asked as Reid climbed atop of the steed without so much as a quick explanation.

"Please let me get there in time! Let it not be too late. I can't lose her!" he desperately pleaded as he pushed the horse onward, faster and faster. *She wouldn't do it...she couldn't,* he tried to reason, *Yes she would! Eibhleann would surely go through with something so rash or drastic!*

The slow incline of the hills were getting steeper and rockier. Reid knew he was nearing their special place on the coast. Once he reached it, his horse barely had time to come to a halt before Reid jumped from it. He ran to the boulder Eibhleann had sat on only days ago. Something on top of it glistened in the sun and gained his attention straight away.

"No...no...." To his horror, he caught sight of his wife's necklace. He picked it up with a trembling hand and stumbled to the edge of the cliff.

She never takes it off...even through our worst arguments. With every terrible thought, fear rose.

"Eibhleann, no...." he gazed over the side and saw the powerful waves crashing against the jagged rocks below. He blinked back the tears to try and focus as it hit him. There was no surviving a fall that great. He was too late. "No!" Reid's heartbraking cry echoed as he fell to his knees. *She's gone...I'm too late!* He clutched her necklace against his chest and wept with everything in him.

All of his hopes of Eibhleann coming to the truth were gone. That very hope had kept him going all those long months during his slow recovery. All that was left was a deep void that gnawed within Reid.

I wish none of this had happened. Anything would have been better than death! If only there had been some warning...something to have led me to believe she would.... "Eibhleann, I'm so sorry!" his agonizing cries sounded forth. The emptiness was so great Reid felt it overtake him as if it could crush him. There was no relief to be found.

Once he had cried all he could, Reid slowly got up from the ground and up onto his knees again. What was he to do now? He didn't want to get up, not wanting to accept Eibhleann's death.

There's nothing I can do now. She's gone...I've lost her forever. Reid tried to make sense of something, anything. He felt numb, other than the pounding in his head and the sorrow in his heart. He forced himself to his feet. There was nothing to do but make his way back to his horse and go home. The temptation to do as Eibhleann had done and take his own life, was growing stronger all the time. He had to leave before he surrendered to it.

"She's not dead," a voice spoke to his heart. It stopped Reid in his tracks. He quickly pushed it aside and climbed onto the horse. *"She's not dead."*

It's only wishful thinking, Reid thought.

"Eibhleann is not dead. She's alive! the voice got even stronger. Reid was instantly brought back to the first time he'd seen his wife with another man, down the street from the pub. He could almost hear Eibhleann laughing in the man's arms.

The man is a captain, he reasoned.

"You know Eibhleann and what she is capable of." When he eventually allowed himself to consider what the inward voice was saying, Reid thought more carefully on such an obscure idea. *Eibhleann is just bold enough to do such a despicable thing as this.* Reid struggled through the grief that surrounded him to find a very small glimmer of hope. *There's only one way to find out.*

CHAPTER EIGHTEEN

*T*he door creaked open and a wealthy gentleman walked in. Several people gawked at him as he made his way to the barkeep.

"Have you seen Lady Kerrich at all?" Reid inquired. As soon as he spoke in hushed tones, the few men sitting at the bar listened intently.

"Who?" the barkeep asked.

"Oh...I meant to say Eibhleann, Eibhleann O'Breen...has she been here at all?"

"An' who might yar be?" the barkeep swiftly exchanged glances with a man sitting to the left of Reid, trying to go unnoticed. Reid however, didn't miss a thing.

"Lord Kerrich, her husband, wants to know!" Reid snapped angrily. Who did this barkeep think he was? Reid was in a terrible hurry to get to Eibhleann, and these low lives were slowing him down. "Well? Have you seen her?" his voice grew louder in his impatience.

"Hey nigh," the man beside Reid spoke slowly as if mocking his urgency. He stood up. "Now perhaps we've seen her...." Reid swiftly looked at the barkeep. What were these two conspiring? The man behind the bar appeared to be trying to mask his amusement. "And maybe we 'aven't. It's really up to yer." Reid glanced back at the person in front of him and saw his outstretched hand, waiting for payment. Reid, already seething, was now furious! Instead of giving the worthless man anything, he roughly grabbed him by the collar and pulled him closer to him.

"Where is my wife?" The entire room grew quiet at his sudden outburst.

"Alright! Alright! I don't nu!" Reid wasn't satisfied with his answer. The man at the end of Reid's grip became serious at last and cowered.

"What of the captain? Captain McNeil? Tell me!" he tightened his hold on the man's collar.

"He set sail this mornin'."

"Where is he headed?"

"Ter 'is next shipment...the port in Boston."

Now that Reid had gotten the much needed information, he quickly released the man, causing him to stumble over the stool behind him and fall backwards onto the ground. Reid left the pub at once. He had much to do.

CHAPTER NINTEEN

"  hat's wrong with you tonight?" Captain McNeil asked as they walked arm in arm down the street. The pub had just closed so they decided to go for a walk before going their separate ways. "You seem much quieter than usual and sang only sullen songs."

"Oh nothin'," Eibhleann sighed. McNeil then stopped.

"Now this isn't like you at all. What's wrong, love?" he reached over, under her chin and gently raised her head upward until she met his gaze. Eibhleann really didn't feel like discussing it.

"Is it that bloody husband of yours?" She didn't say a word in reply but the despairing look in her eyes in the bright moonlight revealed all. "So it is him…I hate knowing the pain he causes you. Won't you let me have my men rough him up a bit to teach him a lesson?" Eibhleann felt McNeil's arm grow tense in anger. "No, I'm fine...just tired av dealin' with him."

"Then don't. Come away with me like I've been sayin' for the last few weeks. Be rid of the fool for good," McNeil suggested.

"I can't. It's loike I've towl ya over and over. Ya don't nu him. He's used ter gettin' his way. He wud never let me leave Ireland," she tried to explain and began walking again. McNeil slowly followed.

"He wouldn't have to know," McNeil continued. A single thought immediately crossed Eibhleann's mind the moment he said it.

"What?" he asked when she came to a stop. "What is it?"

"I jist got an idea."

"Such as?"

"Well, it might 'elp us ter be free from him...forever."

"Tell me what it is," he asked again but Eibhleann didn't answer right away. She was deep in thought while constructing a plan.

"Yes...it jist moight work......"

The St. Carlin

Eibhleann thought back over that evening. Though she felt relieved to be away from Reid for good, and bound to America, she couldn't help wonder about her decision. It wasn't like her at all to consider her actions. At first, she was excited about her new adventure, yet when she woke up on the ship, she couldn't stop thinking about Reid. She knew he had seen her misleading note by now. She lay on the bed and looked around the extravagant cabin. The rich wood moldings were as grand as some of the rooms at Saerlaith. It even had a small sitting room between the bedroom and the captain's small office.

I have everything I could want here, Eibhleann thought. She hated the way she felt. She just wanted to be free of the nagging thoughts of her husband. Eibhleann hoped leaving would release her from them. Try as she might to push away her persistent thoughts, they kept coming back.

What did Reid do when he read it? What is he doing right now? Is he sad over it? Does he really believe me to be dead? "Enough!" She sighed. She quickly got out of bed to get dressed and hopefully get her mind off of Reid. It took a bit longer then she was used to without the help of her ladies maid. That was one thing she missed already. She had more than enough help for anything she might need since marrying her wealthy husband.

Eibhleann finally fastened the last tricky button behind her back before going to the mirror. It sat on top of a white vanity McNeil bought her. The minute she sat down to start on her hair, the troubling thoughts caught up to her.

"What's wrong with me?" she mumbled, "Forget aboyt him an' concentrate on your new life!" she tried to convince herself by looking herself in the eye in the mirror and telling herself aloud. Just then there was a knock on the door.

"Come in." McNeil opened it and casually entered.

"Are you finished gettin' ready?"

"Jist aboyt," Eibhleann didn't turn away from the mirror as she combed her hair. She then pulled it up and secured it with a decorative flower.

McNeil came up behind her until she could see him in the mirror also.

"You look stunning," he stated. Eibhleann smiled as her concerns melted away one by one.

"There…all ready," she finally turned to the captain. He took her hand in his, raised it up to his lips, and kissed it.

"I've never been happier havin' you here with me."

"Nor I," she sighed.

"The crew is just as pleased to have someone such as yourself aboard. They eagerly wait to hear you sing."

"Shall we go out an' meet them?"

"Aye, tonight we celebrate for an angel is with us," McNeil gently pulled Eibhleann to her feet.

CHAPTER TWENTY

Ireland   *April 1816*

arrick entered the crowded pub and found a seat. As he waited for someone to take his order, he looked around the room for a familiar face. Through the smoke of several men, puffing on their pipes, Garrick scanned the people sitting at the bar. He didn't usually frequent the less esteemed pubs in the small Irish towns, for he despised the Irish. There were plenty of better and more respectable establishments where likeminded British men, such as he, preferred to go. Garrick would have gone there instead but it was already late and this pub was the closest to where he was currently residing.

Another reason why he carefully searched out everyone's faces was to be sure he didn't know anyone there. He wanted to be free to drink in peace. Just then, one of the men at the bar stood to take off his jacket.

Roland Carver? What is he doing here? Garrick asked himself. He couldn't hold back his curiosity for long so he finally got up and sauntered over to him.

"What is Saerlaith's steward doing here? And during the week no less?"

"Master Rigby…." Roland very nearly choked and instantly stiffened at the sight of him. Garrick figured the man felt the same as he in not wanting to be seen at the lowly place. "Haven't seen the likes of you for a long time either," Roland nervously motioned to the empty seat beside him just as a pint was set in front of him.

"Is it a new day off or something?" Garrick didn't let up as he sat down. After Roland took a long sip, he replied, "I was discharged."

"Really? You were let go?"

"By your fool of a—" he quickly stopped and glanced at Garrick. He had done the unthinkable in speaking of the lord that way.

"You don't have to guard your words around me…especially when referring to Reid. I have no regard towards him. In fact, sounds like you share my thoughts." Roland was set at ease upon hearing this. He wasn't overly surprised by Garrick's statement. He had witnessed the tension between the brothers often in years past.

"So my fool of a brother fired you. What are your plans now?" Garrick asked just as his drink was brought to him.

"I don't know yet. I'm almost glad to be rid of him. All of his generosity and kindness toward the Irish was starting to make me sick. When it all comes down to it, we were probably losing more money than anything…all for those worthless, good for nothing—" Roland stopped ranting when he remembered they were in a pub, surrounded by Irish.

"Well, since you don't have any prospects as of yet, I might have something," Garrick leaned forward to speak to the steward more privately to reveal what he had in mind.

CHAPTER TWENTY-ONE

The St. Carlin   *June 1816*

Eibhleann entered the cabin and slammed the door behind her as hard as she could. She angrily paced the small sitting area in the room.

"Oh...infuriatin' man!" she huffed. The worst part was, she couldn't get far. The ship was getting smaller and smaller in the two months that had passed.

It wasn't long before Eibhleann heard the inevitable knock at the door.

"What?" she sighed with irritation. The door opened and McNeil came inside.

"Why are ya in here? We're all waiting."

"Aye, well...." Eibhleann tried to come up with an excuse.

"Well what? I told them you were going to sing."

I don't care what you told them! she thought in her anger.

She managed to bite her tongue, this time anyway. It was getting harder to keep silent.

Eibhleann went over and sat down on the edge of the bed.

"I'm actually not feelin' up ter it," she innocently gazed up at McNeil.

"But I told them you would," he argued.

"I don't care!" she blurted for her temper got the better of her at last. McNeil's face instantly grew red.

"I said I told them you would sing tonight. What I say is what is done," his voice lowered as he stepped closer and looked down at her as though to intimidate her. To his surprise, Eibhleann met his gaze head on and boldly rose to her feet. She was completely undaunted.

"An' I said I don't care." She seemed to smirk at him, daring him to do something about it. He was now boiling over. He could hardly speak much less think straight. No one had ever stood up to him like this, especially a woman. Who did she think she was?

They stared each other down for a few moments before McNeil broke the silence.

"What would you have me do? I gave my word as the captain." Eibhleann still did not waver at this.

"I thought ya loved me…more than your word," she calmly stated in a conniving and impudent tone.

"I'll give you one more chance," McNeil bypassed her absurd statement and spoke to her like he would one of his sailors with a sharp demand and booming voice. It was as if he was scolding a child. It was something Eibhleann loathed most of all. She laughed in his face then moved to sit at her vanity.

"You can give me al' the chances ya loike…I will not be singin'," she reached up and began taking the hair pins out of her hair.

McNeil did all he could not to go up to her and strike her. Instead, he quickly conjured up a scheme that would surely hurt her much worse than he could.

She'll be sorry for going against me, he happily thought to himself as he walked to the door. Eibhleann's back was turned towards him so she thought he was leaving. Instead, he opened the door and called for his men.

"Bart, Sam, get in here!"

What does he think he's doing? Too scared to deal with me himself, is he? Eibhleann thought and even smiled to herself. She calmly pulled out the last pin, causing her hair to fall around her shoulders.

"Aye, Captain?"

"Take this worthless lass to the brig." The sailors gave McNeil a confused look just as Eibhleann glanced at them in shock. When they saw that the captain was serious, Bart and Sam quickly heeded the order. The two men approached and each took a gentle hold of Eibhleann's arms.

"What chucker ya think you're doin'? How dare ya treat me in such a fashion!" They dragged her to the door. McNeil ignored her and only spoke to the men.

"Ya don't have to treat her like the lady of the ship...not anymore."

"Unhand me! Ya can't do this," Eibhleann shrieked.

CHAPTER TWENTY-TWO

ibhleann heard someone come towards the brig. She stood to her feet and grasped the cold bars. *Has McNeil finally come to his senses?* "'ave ya come to release me?" she asked. The sailor shook his head. "To brin' me food then?"

"Captain says you don't deserve food. Not until you apologize to him," he replied. Eibhleann folded her arms in stubbornness. "I came to tell you just that."

"What an eejit," she mumbled under her breath.

"I guess it might be awhile then," he stated the obvious and turned to leave when Eibhleann hurridly spoke up.

"Oh, don't go yet...please."

"Why?" the sailor stopped and glanced at her.

"Come 'ere." As he stepped back to the brig, Eibhleann went closer to the bars and leaned against them. "Ya know...I 'aven't towl anyone this but I took notice of ya the moment I came aboard the ship."

"Me?" the man seemed shocked, precisely what she wanted.

"Why not yer? You're strong, tall, an' pure handsome." She put every effort in her flirtatious ways as she slowly reached out between the bars and retied the small red neckerchief he wore about his neck. He barely breathed. "Perhaps I've been the fool in not sayin' so earlier an' continuin' with McNeil. Anyone with eyes can see you're the better paddy."

"Well...I am about to be promoted to an officer," the sailor proudly stated. It only showed that he was hanging on to her every manipulative word.

"Is that so?" Eibhleann tried to sound interested. In truth, she could care less about him. "Pity you're not the captain. You shud be."

"Ah, now you're makin' me embarrassed."

"Seein' as we've gotten more acquainted nigh, I 'ope we can 'av more talks loike this and git to nu each other better. Want to know somethin'?"

"What?"

"Do you know what wud please me?" Because it was obvious that the ignorant sailor was hopelessly infatuated and under her spell, she was confident in her plan.

"What is it?"

"Moight you consider sneakin' some food with you the next time ya come?" Eibhleann finally asked.

"But the captain...."

"At least a bit av water...it 'as been an entire day without anythin', ya know." Under normal circumstances, Eibhleann wouldn't have been so blunt in making her request known so quickly, but she was so hungry and thirsty. She couldn't be any more subtle for she was too desperate.

"Well, I don't know," the sailor fought with the idea.

"I wud really loike it," Eibhleann tried to make her voice sound as sweetly as she could.

"I...can't." That was it. She couldn't hide her true motive

any longer.

"Ah cum on, ya coward. It's simple enoof!" she snapped.

"No, and I'll have no more of your wiling ways." Eibhleann sighed in frustration at his response. He quickly made his way down the hall and out of sight.

For the first time in her life, Eibhleann felt fear rise up in her. Never had her efforts been turned down nor control taken from her.

What should I do now? she couldn't help but ask herself. Though she was much too strong willed to admit, she wondered if she ever should have come against McNeil.

The next three days were the longest days Eibhleann had ever known. She was able to get a very small piece of bread and even a bit of water from another doltish sailor, who was completely oblivious to her scheme. However, the boredom of being kept inside the brig was more than she could bear. Eibhleann eventually broke down and told another sailor to fetch the captain. She had no real intention of apologizing to McNeil, yet she thought when he saw her, he might change his mind somehow.

"I thought you might be feeling differently by now," McNeil arrogantly walked up to the brig. "I heard you are ready to apologize."

"An' what if I am?" Eibhleann had to choke back how she truly felt, for the time being.

McNeil motioned to the nearby sailor to unlock the brig. In truth, he was surprised at how long it had taken her to call for him. He marveled at how well she looked for someone who hadn't been given food or water for three days, or so he thought.

Eibhleann's knees wobbled with weakness and she felt dizzy as she stepped out but she endeavored to appear confident and unafraid of the captain's presence. She met his gaze and found a smug grin on his face as he waited for her to speak. The last thing Eibhleann wanted to do was give in to his absurd wishes, yet what else could she do?

"I await your apology," McNeil pushed further, causing her anger to rise.

"I...." her mouth felt as if it was filled with sand as she considered actually being forced to go through with this. There was no escaping it. Eibhleann glanced to the wooden floor and constrained herself forward. "I regret...me actions the other night...an' I apologize." She shut her eyes tightly and agonizingly listened to McNeil gloat unmercifully.

"There now, was that so hard?" he spewed. He then reached out, put his hand under her chin, and raised it so she would look up at him. "In the future, you would be wise to try a bit harder to please me. Your efforts have been wanting of late." Now he had gone too far, especially when he moved in closer to kiss her. Eibhleann's face immediately grew warm in her rage. She couldn't stand any more of this and would rather starve. She instantly drew what little strength she could muster and slapped McNeil across the face.

"Ya wish me to try 'arder do ya? Ya 'aven't seen anythin' yet, you...you brute!" Eibhleann shouted and was planning to hit him again. McNeil quickly recovered his surprise and caught her by her unkempt hair.

"I knew you wouldn't yield... but you will!" he dragged her back to the brig and threw her inside with much force. She fell hard against the plank floor. Her chin and the lower part of her face burned painfully from scraping it.

"You'll be sorry!" he continued to shout as he began to leave. Eibhleann covered her throbbing face and watched him leave through blurred vision.

By the next day, Eibhleann was so weak she could barely stand. Her chin and lips were swollen and chapped from the layer of blood that had dried. She couldn't even try to persuade anyone for food for no one came. She slowly drifted off to sleep when a noise caused her to stir. It was someone coming through the hall. She did all she could to lift her head to see who it was. The sailor said nothing as he unlocked the door and stepped inside.

"Wat do ya want?" Eibhleann whispered hoarsely. Her mouth was so dry she could hardly form words.

"Ya have to come with me to the deck."

"Why?" she winced for it was painful to even speak.

"Come on," he bent down to help her up and nearly had to carry her to the deck.

Eibhleann had become so incoherent, she hadn't noticed they had docked in Boston. It wasn't until she was brought on deck that she took in the large, noisy harbor.

"Here she is now." She swiftly became more alert when she heard McNeil's voice. She saw him talking to another man. Though he never looked at her, McNeil still wore the haughty smirk.

"What's goin' on?" Eibhleann asked but was ignored.

"She may look helpless but she can be quite difficult. She's a feisty one," McNeil went on.

"She won't be any problem. We deal with difficult ones often enough. She'll soon break...if she's smart," the other man replied.

"Bart, ya might as well bring her to this man's carriage."

"Aye, aye, Captain."

"What's goin' on? Where are ya takin' me?" Eibhleann grew louder with fright. She was much too weak to try and stop the sailor from carrying her off of the St. Carlin.

CHAPTER TWENTY-THREE

Boston, Massachusetts

eid stepped off the gangplank and took in all of Boston. He began to feel a bit overwhelmed by it. *Where do I even begin my search?* he asked himself and gazed passed the bustling harbor and into the city. "Lord, you've led me this far. Please guide my steps," he prayed under his breath.

Reid's first move was to visit the Princeton Shipping Company, for the despised Captain McNeil worked for them. Reid didn't really know how long McNeil and Eibhleann planned to be in town but he would find out all he could. There wasn't one second that Reid thought he might be wasting his time by coming all this way. His sole purpose was to find his wife.

Once Reid's footman arranged for a carriage, he was on his way to the shipping company.

"The man you need to talk to is right in there."

"Thank you." Reid made his way inside one of the several large storage buildings owned by The Princeton Shipping Company. Just like the man had instructed, there was the person Reid was searching for. He dearly hoped the man could give him at least some information that would lead him closer to Eibhleann.

"Excuse me," Reid's voice echoed in the vast building to the man who's back was turned toward him. When he heard it, he turned to Reid and squinted. "One of your men told me you could help me," Reid continued and directly went over to him.

"Aye?" the man replied but returned his gaze down to the papers he held in his hand.

"Do you have a moment? I have some questions."

"What's this all about?" he gruffly asked and finally glanced at Reid. He immediately seemed to put up his defenses.

"There's no problem...I just need to find out some information about one of your ships."

"Alright?" the sternness subsided a bit.

"Unfortunately, I don't know the name of the vessel but the captain is John McNeil. When did he arrive in Boston?" The man eyed Reid curiously at his question but eventually answered after paging through his log.

"About a fortnight ago."

"And has he already set sail again?" Reid apprehensively asked. Two weeks was longer than he'd expected to hear. He had hoped they would still be in town.

"Yes." Reid's expectations instantly tempted to fall.

"Oh…did you happen to overhear anything such as if Captain McNeil planned to do anything out of the ordinary before he left?" *This can't be it! There has to be more he can tell me!* Something inside Reid urged him forward.

"Uh…not really. I guess I do remember him asking me where the nearest factory was," he answered.

Factory? What ever for? "Might I ask what your answer was?" Reid could tell the man was growing tired of his persistent inquiries.

"I told him it was the Lessing Mill. It's a textile factory just west of here. Is that all because I should be getting back to it?"

"Yes, thank you for your time," Reid turned to leave. He made his way out of the shipping yard and back to his carriage.

"Did you find out anything, My Lord?" Eli, Reid's footman, asked.

"Just about a factory," Reid sighed in frustration. *Oh well, if this is the only thing to stand on, it's worth looking into it further,* his determination stirred. "Well, let's go to it. It's called Lessing Mill," he directed his footman, who in turn told the driver.

The entire time it took to get to the factory, Reid fought within himself.

Why would McNeil want to know about a factory? What am I doing here? Eibhleann obviously chose McNeil over me. She'll never listen if I do find her. They're surely long gone by now. It was the same string of doubts he'd dealt with for the long journey from Ireland. He couldn't help but feel discouraged as all of the uncertainty seemed to pile over him.

The grim looking factory came into view. The tall gate was open so they drove through it. Once they came to a halt, Reid walked up to the entrance. He was directly shown to an office by an aloof maid and was told to wait for the person in charge.

Reid was left to inspect the room. The room wasn't overly large. There were two desks at both sides of the it, facing each other. The room was plain enough, yet someone had put just enough effort into the decorating to show their business was thriving, such as fancy rugs and leather chairs.

Reid carefully took in every detail while he waited. He didn't see anything of concern or out of the ordinary, yet something told him otherwise. Reid couldn't figure out why but there was a queer feeling in the pit of his stomach. Something wasn't right.

The grandfather clock suddenly chimed and made him jump.
"Lord, what is it? What's going on here?" he took this opportunity of being alone to whisper. "Is this some sort of warning...telling me to leave?" No, that wasn't it. *What else could this uneasiness mean?* Reid no longer had time to think as the door opened and two men entered. One was a plump man with a short beard, while the other was tall, wiry, and wore spectacles. They each were dressed in suits. They looked at Reid strangely at first, without saying a word. It was almost as if they were weighing him inquisitively. It only caused Reid's anxiousness to worsen.

"Hello," Reid finally broke the silence.
"The maid said you needed to speak to someone in charge," the taller of the two coldly stated.
"Yes, I...." At that moment, something came over Reid and told him what he must do to protect himself and find out more of what was truly going on. "I'm uh...interested in your fine establishment here...perhaps as a sort of an investor." This caused both men to change their odd behavior instantly. Instead of being unfriendly any longer, they changed their tune in a hurry.
"Why, yes...." the taller exchanged glances with the other.

"Won't you have a seat over here? I'm Otto Bayes," he extended his hand to Reid, as did the other man.

"I'm Byron Lessing. And you are?" Reid hesitated in his reply. He couldn't very well tell him his real name in case they might know it. It wouldn't do any good to have them recognize his name as the person who helped the Irish into parliament, especially when something strange might be going on. People in America didn't treat the Irish any better than in Europe. However, he didn't exactly want to lie. He had to think quickly!

"I am Lord Reid Lennox, Marquess of Kelvin." He had been named after his uncle so he used the territory name as his for the time being.

"Let's have a seat, shall we?" When they were all seated, more questions arose.

"What brings you to Boston all the way from England?" Mr. Lessing asked and made a presumption from Reid's accent.

"I merely wanted a change. I've only just arrived but I'm very interested in your industry here," Reid began but treaded very lightly. He had to choose his words carefully. He tried not to miss a thing so he could figure out what was behind the situation. "I can see you run a fine business and I can already tell its run efficiently by intelligent people, such as yourselves. I want to be a part of it." Reid watched as they gladly took in every bit of flattery. They were undoubtingly very proud of themselves.

"We're always open to investors. I'll admit we don't get them as often as we would like, especially someone of your honored position," Lessing stated. At first Reid worried they might see through his charade but now he knew there would be no problem.

"I suppose the first step to getting better acquainted would be to show you around," Mr. Bayes stood.

"Splendid," Reid replied and followed their lead. The true reason for his visit was now presenting itself. He had to find out if his wife or the captain was there or not, or at least find out why they wished to come here.

They led him to several different work areas. Reid soon noticed that the majority of the rooms were locked. Bayes and Lessing didn't seem at all nervous as they unlocked each door and let Reid have a look inside. The people, hard at work, were of various ages of both men and women. He was surprised to find some children as young as the age of six working among the others. He had never been inside a factory before so he didn't quite know if this was common or not. However, another thing that bothered Reid was the work conditions. It was extremely hot in the cramped rooms and some people didn't look healthy at all. Room after room was the same.

While on their way to yet another floor in the tall factory to see more rooms, someone came up to the two men in charge.

"Sir, something has come up that I must discuss with you."

"Can't you see we're busy at the moment?" Mr. Bayes snorted. Both he and Mr. Lessing seemed overly aggravated by the interruption.

"Don't worry about me. I can wait," Reid spoke up to try and help things. To give them some privacy, he strolled to the end of the hall to wait for them before climbing the next set of stairs. They spoke in hushed tones but Reid didn't mind it in the least. It gave him more time to take in his surroundings. He immediately caught sight of a door to his left with a padlock on it. Unlike all the other rooms, this was unlocked. Reid glanced down the hall to see if all was clear. Sure enough, the men were still deep in conversation. He quietly opened the door a little. He had to squint to make out anything inside the dark room. There were several beds scattered on the floor. Now Reid was more confused than ever.

Are people residing here or...are they being forced to stay against their will? he asked himself. The exterior of the door looked as if it was locked frequently.

"Sorry about the wait." Reid was startled by Mr. Lessing.

"Uh...yes," his head jerked up as he hurriedly closed the

door. He could see that Lessing noticed his anxiousness and waited for him to say something about it. *Surely he'll suspect something amiss now. Did I ruin my chances?* Reid held his breath as he waited for Lessing to speak.

"Shall we?" Lessing eyed him suspiciously and slowly motioned the way to the stairs. It made Reid all the more nervous when he didn't say more.

He had to have seen me! What is going on here?

Everyone in the room stiffened when the door was unlocked then opened. No one dared to anger whoever was checking in on them by doing anything wrong. Anyone who might not have seen the door opened was swiftly warned by the others. No one wanted to risk it. Sure enough, the two owners walked in a little ways. The people nearest to the door held their breath as they carefully peaked at them for a swift look to see what their intent for coming was. It was then that a third person entered behind them.

Reid was pretending to be truly interested in the extravagant details coming from Bayes and Lessing when they were abruptly interposed.

"Get back to work!" A man shouted, followed by a shriek. He shoved a woman to the floor right before them. The woman glanced up at the three men and appeared quite startled and almost confounded at what had just happened. She quickly looked away and rubbed her stinging hands from the fall. The man who pushed her was a guard of some kind and must have missed seeing the door open and the two owners now present. He stepped forward to yell at the woman further but abruptly stopped. His eyes widened when he saw who was witnessing his brash actions.

"Oh, I'm sorry sirs," his tone drastically changed.

"Don't just stand there…in front of our important guest. Get her up and move along!" Lessing lectured sharply. The man, who worked for them, roughly grabbed the woman's arm and lifted her from the floor. He then took her away, out of sight. As he did, the homely woman managed to look back at Reid and caught his gaze for a brief moment.

Reid could only glance at Bayes and Lessing, shaken by the horrendous act. They both appeared as if nothing out of the ordinary had taken place.

Does this violence happen often? he asked himself. He had to hide his stunned reaction, especially when he realized they were watching. He did his very best to look uncaring as the two owners did, but inside, Reid could barely contain himself.

"Pardon the interruption, Lord Kelvin. Please, let's continue this way," Bayes suggested.

The moment he heard the door close, the man spoke.

"You made me look like a fool!"

"And jist how did I chucker that?" Eibhleann snapped before she could stop herself or think of what she was saying. The man took ahold of her upper arm and jerked her closer. Eibhleann winced at his roughness.

"Don't speak to me that way!" he growled in her face, "That kind of talk will get you locked up. Do you want to go without food and water once again?"

"No," she whispered but he wasn't satisfied with her response.

"I can easily go and tell them that you're gettin' out of hand," he threatened.

"Naw, please!" she begged.

"Alright then…get back to work!" he shouted and shoved her back to her spot.

Eibhleann's eyes burned as she tried to hold back the tears. *He looked right at me…but he didn't know me,* she recalled the very brief moment their eyes had met. Reid's gaze held no recognition for her. He only stood, watching the ordeal unfold, not knowing what was truly going on. When she had seen Reid walk in behind the cruel factory owners, she couldn't believe it. It was impossible. She didn't think she would ever see him again, muchless in the factory of all places. Her dumbfounded shock was what had gotten her in trouble and caught by the guard.

Her first inclination upon being thrown to the floor was being ashamed at her disheveled appearance. But now, with how close she had been to him, she was upset that he hadn't recognized her. *He could have gotten me out of here! Why couldn't he have known it was me?* she reached up to wipe a tear away. Another thought suddenly struck her when she pulled her hand away from her face. She took in how dirty it was from the hard work she was forced to endure. Her hands and arms weren't the only thing. Eibhleann reached up and touched her course hair. *What if he did know?* The thought crossed her mind. This question was the worst of all. *Oh…why did he have to come? What if he knew it was me but was too stunned by my appearance to want me?* Eibhleann had always been prideful when it came to her looks. *It could just be that he doesn't want me at all…I did after all make him think I was dead. I lied to him so many times…and to make him think I was dead? He could never forgive me.*

Eibhleann returned to her duties, completely hopeless. All she could do was resign herself to never escaping the horrible conditions at the factory.

Reid managed to finish the tour and told them he would think about their financial opportunity. He then quickly left and made his way to his carriage. He didn't want anything to appear indifferent so he forced himself to walk slowly to keep his resolve.

Reid kept his gaze on the carriage before him. Eli stood outside of it, holding the door open for him.

"Did you—" Eli started to ask.

"I need a moment," Reid interrupted tersely and climbed inside. The footman closed the door and Reid was finally alone and away from prying eyes, before he broke down completely. He couldn't stop the angry tears that stung his eyes, nor the rage that caused him to shake.

When he had seen her, Reid had almost lost it completely. At first, he hadn't recognized her poor condition at all, but when she had glanced back at him while being taken away, he saw it. It was Eibhleann. Seeing her beaten and bruised was very nearly his undoing, especially with how she was treated before his eyes. It was indeed the hardest thing he'd ever done to stop himself from doing something then and there. But he couldn't have. It would have put her safety, as well as his own, at risk. No, he would have to do something else about it. Now he was very glad he'd followed his heart. There was no doubt something was terribly wrong going on in the factory.

Knowing his wife was in their hands and at their mercy only made it more difficult to think clearly. What should his next move be? How could he get help?

Lord, You've led me so far. Keep showing me the way. Thank You for helping me find Eibhleann. Now help me get her out of there!

CHAPTER TWENTY-FOUR

 nd what is your concern exactly?"

"I have reason to believe they are keeping people there against their will," Reid explained to the authorities.

"Did you actually see the things you speak of first hand?"

"Yes," he sighed in frustration. This was getting him nowhere. "I saw a room filled with beds with a lock on the door. As for the cruel treatment, I saw it before my very eyes." Reid watched the officer think on what he had said. He was sure the law enforcement would do something about it straight away. It was what Reid was accustomed to. What he said was quickly carried out without question, that is, everyone but the English.

"Well, thank you for your concern." Unfortunately, the officer leaned back in his chair and slowly replied. He more or less disregarded everything Reid had told him. "We'll keep your concerns in mind.

"So you're not going to do anything about this?" Reid asked, incredulous.

"This factory has been here a long time and no one has ever come to us about this matter."

"Are you saying I'm making all of this up?" Reid was trying his best to remain calm but his voice was growing louder.

"I'm only saying we have everything well taken care of." It was then Reid realized what was truly going on. There was nothing more to be said so he stood.

"Thank you for your time," he sighed.

As soon as he left, Reid's thoughts awoke to formulate his next move for this proved to be a complete waste of time. He was now convinced that the authorities were a part of whatever the factory was up to.

What can I do? I'm alone in this.

"Did they heed you, My Lord?" Eli opened the carriage door when Reid approached.

"Not at all," he replied in defeat.

"They won't do anything?"

"No. It appears to be up to us now."

Eli took in the factory from behind a nearby tree. In the moonlight he scanned the building until he found the window Reid told him about. It was the only small window that was close to the ground.

He took a deep breath before bolting toward the building. His first obstacle was the gate. It was taller than he was and made of thick iron bars. Eli was an agile young man. He backed up to make a run for it and easily climbed over it as quietly as possible then crept to the window. Wooden shutters covered it and it was locked with an old, rusted padlock. Eli tried to slow his swift breathing and his heart that was beating wildly from his fervency. He had to stop his shaking hands to concentrate on the lock. He reached into his pocket and got the small wire for this very purpose. It took a bit longer in the dark but soon Eli smiled to himself when the lock clicked opened. The shutters covering the window opened easily enough as he continued to go unnoticed. It was even darker as he slowly peered inside. Reid might have told him about the window but that was the extent of it. He didn't know what awaited him inside.

Eli's breath was now shaky with facing the unknown. He couldn't wait forever so he ducked down and quickly climbed inside. The room turned out to be a storage room filled with boxes and crates. All he could do now was find the door and hope it wasn't locked from the outside.

He stumbled his way through the black room and to the door. He reached up to turn the handle and was relieved to find it unlocked. He opened it very slowly. Because he didn't hear anyone, he carefully looked out. He found nothing but an empty and dimly lit hallway.

This is proving to be an easy task, he thought to himself. Just then Eli heard a noise. He spun around to find no one. *What was that?* he looked around to locate it when it stopped. *What could it be?* He froze and scanned the different doors that lined the hall. There it was again and this time he recognized the sound. It was someone coughing and it was coming through a door directly to his left. Step by step Eli crept to it. As he neared it he saw that it was locked. He then heard the cough again along with other people. He got close enough until he put his ear against the door.

Lord Kerrich was right. It sounds like quite a few people are in there.

Eli took one last look in both directions of the hall before reaching for the wire in his pocket again. He was just starting to pick the lock when a voice was heard from behind.

"What do you think you're doing?"

CHAPTER TWENTY-FIVE

*R*eid apprehensively waited at the hotel for Eli to return with Eibhleann. It only grew later and later with no sign of them. He was beginning to grow concerned. There were so many things that could go wrong. At first Reid felt guilty by having Eli find his wife for him but he didn't want to jeopardize their efforts all together. He would be recognized straight away while Eli on the other hand had a better chance in case their plan failed. Furthermore, Eli was more than willing to help in any way possible. But now Reid was having second thoughts on the plans he'd made.

The night wore on with still no footman. Reid ended up staying awake through the night. However, in the last few hours before dawn, he must have finally dozed off because when the clock struck eight o'clock, Reid awoke on the couch in the sitting room. When he realized it was morning, he shot to his feet and went searching for Eli. To his dismay, he was nowhere to be found. Reid tried not to fear the worst as he quickly got ready to go to the factory himself and hoped he could somehow, find out more.

He prayed until he reached it and almost hesitantly went to the front entrance. Part of him felt as if he was walking into a trap, yet there was no other way to find out.

"Lord Kelvin, nice to see you again," Mr. Lessing greeted him after the maid led Reid into the office.

"And you as well," Reid apprehensively replied. He forced himself to act as if nothing was amiss. He also tried to gauge how the owners acted. Mr. Lessing didn't get up but remained seated at the desk, which Reid thought was a bit strange. Mr. Bayes, who stood near the desk, extended his hand to him.

"Have you thought anymore about our business venture?" Bayes asked.

"I have," Reid strained to sound friendly like an idealistic and ignorant young man merely trying to spend his inheritance wisely. "I've slept on it for a few days now and feel inclined to take you up on it." He was starting to feel more at ease now that the owners both smiled upon hearing this. Nothing seemed any different. *Yet what has become of Eli?* That single question remained at the forefront of his mind.

"Splendid," Mr. Lessing finally stood and came around his desk. Reid thought he was going to shake his hand also but he did no such thing. Instead, he motioned his hand toward the open office door, as if signaling someone. "Before we finalize the details, I want to bring your attention to one last thing. We seemed to have overlooked it when you were here last." Reid didn't know what to expect to come through the door, nor did he have much time to. Within seconds, two men, one of which was the rough man Reid had seen before, silently walked in with someone else between them, hunched over. It was Eli! Reid did his best to appear unmoved to protect himself but his footman's poor appearance shocked him. He was badly beaten, so much so, he couldn't stand on his own accord. Panic swiftly rose up in him at the distressing sight. It was completely his fault. Reid didn't know how to act anymore. Did they know the truth? Was Eibhleann safe? Were the owners merely testing him to see if he recognized Eli? Reid quickly decided to remain silent to see what they would do or say next.

"We found him picking a lock," Lessing motioned for the men to bring Eli closer. Mr. Lessing then went up to him, took hold of Eli's hair, and jerked his head up. Eli's face was black and blue with dried blood coming from his nose and other deep wounds. Reid's heart beat quickened with both anger and alarm.

"Tell Lord Kelvin what you shared with us last night," Byron Lessing glanced back at Reid and smiled wryly. Reid now knew what he and Bayes were smiling over before. Eli did his best to meet Reid's gaze, for his one eye was swollen shut.
"I'm sorry, My Lord," his coughed then spoke hoarsely.
"Lord Kelvin, if that's truly your name…your man here was kind enough to inform us of your actual reason for coming," Lessing went on. His delight in having one up on Reid could be heard in his every word.

Reid closed his eyes in defeat just as Lessing signaled toward the door again. This time a man escorted Eibhleann inside. Reid might have been able to hide his astonishment before but his resolve vanished when he saw her. She was barely recognizable. She wore rags and was filthy from head to toe.
"Eibhleann!" he blurted. Protective instinct strongly came over him all at once. He had to hold back the urge to immediately beg for her life. He was ardently ready to do whatever it took, even if it meant his own life.

Eibhleann didn't say anything. She could barely make herself look him in the eye.
"It's indeed all true, I see," Bayes interrupted their troubled musings.

"I didn't mean to deceive you in the least. I have come to obtain my wife and I am ready to pay whatever you like for her freedom." Bayes' eyes widened as he looked at Mr. Lessing and adjusted his spectacles on his face. He opened his mouth to take Reid up on his offer.

"Just wait a minute now," Mr. Lessing beat his partner to it and caused the fear in Reid to worsen. "I don't take kindly to someone misleading and deceiving us. I might have considered what you offered before, but now it's a little different." Lessing put his hands together then raised them to his mouth in thought. He was obviously enjoying the power he now held. Each of their lives were in his hands.

He paced until he stopped in front of Eibhleann.

"So let me see here…."

"My life for hers," Reid assuredly spoke up. Eibhleann's gaze shot up at this and she looked at him in amazement, not believing what he'd just said.

How can he say that? He would give his life for me…after all I've done? she thought as her vision became blurred. "Reid, don't," she cried.

"Be quiet!" Byron Lessing spun around to face Eibhleann and hit her across the face.

"Don't touch my wife!" Reid took action the moment it happened and jumped forward. He took ahold of Lessing's jacket and pulled him away from Eibhleann. Reid merely wanted to get him away from his wife, but he didn't mean for Mr. Lessing to stumble over a chair in front of his desk and to the ground on his back. Lessing turned bright red in his anger as he peered over his belly at Reid.

"Get me up!" he spewed while Mr. Bayes and one of their men helped him to his feet. The other guard released Eibhleann's arm and rushed over to Reid to try and contain him from getting away.

"Bring him here," Mr. Lessing ordered through gritted teeth. The other two men in the room went to help hold Reid. Once he was held firmly, Lessing let Reid have it with a blow to his stomach. Reid doubled over in pain. The men forced Reid to stand up straight and held him tightly so Lessing could do it again.

"Stop it! Leave 'im alone!" Eibhleann screamed but was ignored. When he kept on hitting him over and over again, she decided to try to stop it herself. She rushed up behind Lessing to hold back his arm. Instead of doing any good, Lessing merely shoved her away roughly, causing her to fall against the desk. As she hit it, the lamp atop it, tipped and fell over the side. It burst into flames the moment it hit the floor. No one seemed to notice it until the flames swiftly grew. It was consuming the desk and carpet before going up the side of the wall. Only seconds passed before it was nearly unstoppable.

"Byron!" Mr. Bayes suddenly shouted as if he'd just noticed the fire. Everyone's attention was now on it and they immediately went to work to put it out, releasing Reid in the process. He fell to one knee and winced in pain. He felt the pang of his past wound. He coughed and gasped as he looked up at the flames. Reid knew it was impossible to try to stop it. Everything was more than flammable. He had seen most of the work rooms to know all of the machinery was built of wood. The whole place would surely be engulfed in only a matter of minutes. They had to get out of there and quick.

While the others were frantically trying put out the fire, Reid grabbed Eibhleann by the hand and rushed out of the door with Eli limping behind them. Reid's ribs and stomach burned from the beating he had endured. He had to keep going and get to safety. He forced himself to push through the discomfort to keep running. They ran down the hall to the front entrance. Reid couldn't push aside the thoughts of the people he'd seen during the tour of the factory. There were so many women, children, and elderly inside the locked rooms. What would happen to them if he left? The owners cared nothing for them and would only save themselves. He couldn't get their faces nor the images of what would befall them, out of his mind. He knew it wasn't just his own thoughts speaking to him but a leading to turn back.

"Wait." They were nearly to the door when Reid suddenly spoke and came to a swift halt.

"What's the matter?" Eibhleann asked, panting from all the running. There wasn't time to explain.

"Eli, get her safely away from here! I must go back." As soon as Eli nodded, Reid turned away from the group.

"What? No! We 'av to git out of 'ere!" Eibhleann started after him but Eli caught her arm.

"He said we have to get out!" he struggled with her.

"No...Reid! Cum back," Eibhleann kept her eyes on her husband and helplessly watched him rush back down the hall and around the corner. Eli had to literally drag her outside in obedience to Reid's orders.

"Let me go! It's too fierce...he'll be killed!" she screamed and resisted the footman all she could.

She eventually stopped resisting as they hurried down the front steps and away from the factory. They nearly plowed into one man, who was running toward the burning building. Eibhleann and Eli were able to avoid stumbling into him by moving to the side, only to narrowly miss another person. He was also hurrying to the factory. It wasn't until then that Eli glanced toward the front gate. It was wide open and countless people from seemingly everywhere were coming to help. The entire west side of the building was in flames and the black smoke billowed high above it. Because of the enormity of it, it gained the attention of many.

Eli and Eibhleann had to weave through all the people to make it to the gate when a loud noise was heard. They both glanced back to see a large portion of the factory cave in on itself and the fire instantly envelop it.

"No!" Eibhleann cried out in fear, "Reid...." She felt tugging on her arm again. Eli was trying to urge her onward for there was nothing they could do. Eibhleann saw that he was just as distressed as she by the hopelessness and grief on his face. She felt like she was in a kind of fog but alas, she forced herself to continue on. The thought of never seeing Reid again made Eibhleann begin to sob. She could hardly see where she was going. She soon caught her foot on the root of a tree and toppled over. Before Eibhleann was able to get up, her breath caught within her when she felt someone put their hands around her waist. She feared they were caught! She was gently lifted to her feet before she could see who it was.

"Reid!" she gasped, "You're al' right!" In her relief and joyous state, she threw her arms around him.

"Yes but we must keep going if we're to get away unnoticed!" he replied, out of breath. When they were on their way again, Eibhleann noticed for the first time that Reid was nearly covered with soot from head to toe.

The carriage, Reid had hired, was long gone by now so the three walked down a few blocks. At least they were at a safe distance now so they could move at a slower pace. They came to a main road when he found a carriage for hire. The driver, however, wasn't too sure if he wanted to take them because of their strange sight. Reid was covered in soot and Eibhleann was dressed in a poor, tattered dress with her hair a mess. Above all, Eli was horribly beaten. He quickly changed his mind as soon as Reid pulled out his wallet.

No one spoke for some time after they were well on their way back to the hotel. The enormity of what they'd all gone through and escaped from was beginning to have a chance to sink in.

"Once we arrive at the hotel, I'll send for a doctor. You both need medical attention," Reid eventually broke the silence.

"And you as well, My Lord," Eli quietly suggested. Reid said nothing to disagree with him.

"Yer went back to 'elp everyone locked in the workrooms...didn't ya," Eibhleann said quietly and made herself meet his gaze. After being overjoyed to see that he was alright, her shame and regret slowly came over her again. She still couldn't bring herself to believe he came after her and would readily have given his life for her freedom. She didn't quite know how to act now. She felt like she was practically a stranger to him.

"I did, and I wasn't alone. There were other people who came to help. I don't know where they came from but as I was hitting the padlocks with anything I could find, they came and began to help, without saying a word. We were able to get all the doors unlocked then everyone ran for the nearest escape. It seems we weren't the only ones who knew what was going on there."

"We saw people running toward the building as we were leaving," Eli stated.

Eibhleann silently watched Reid pull out his handkerchief to wipe his face. She was again taken back by Reid's heroic and selfless actions.

I've been such a fool, she thought.

CHAPTER TWENTY-SIX

July 1816

he rest of their stay in Boston consisted of Eibhleann's recovery. She slept almost constantly for days. The stress she had gone through deemed to be more than even she had first thought. The treatment she had endured from Captain McNeil was one thing. The factory was a whole other matter. After being taken there, she immediately did what was normal to her and defied and rebelled against the authority. The idea of working under the less than pleasurable conditions did not suit her. She was used to being waited on as a marchioness, but her stubborn and spoiled ways were not put up with for one minute, although it might have taken her longer to realize it. She was simply dealt with as many others had at the factory. Eibhleann was locked up all alone for days. She was starved and beaten before it finally broke her and she complied to work and do what she was told.

Eibhleann's sleep was so deep she easily lost track of time and even days. She could barely recall eating the meals brought to her by her ladies maid, nor being examined by the doctor every few days. Once in a while she could hear quiet conversation going on around her, yet she couldn't focus enough to realize who it was or what it was about. One voice stuck out to her above all others. It was Reid, who would sit by her side.

Is it only a dream or is he truly here with me? she asked herself in her incoherent and passing thoughts. *But it couldn't be a dream,* she reassured when she could feel the warmth of his hand holding hers
"Thank You for bringing her back to me." Eibhleann listened to the tenderness in Reid's voice as he prayed. "I love you, Eibhleann." It was hardly more than a whisper. It seemed to sooth her. She could only catch bits and pieces. Eibhleann willed herself to wake up but as hard as she tried, her eye lids were too heavy and sleep too strong as it pulled her into its peaceful rest.

One particular morning, as she slept, Eibhleann could sense someone's presence in the room.
It must be Alison, she guessed. She opened her eyes just as whoever it was, quietly closed the door behind them. Eibhleann didn't get up but looked around the room. Her thoughts were foggy as she tried to figure out what time it was, though she barely knew what day it was. At that moment, voices could be heard outside her room. She sat up and strained to hear who it was.
"How is she today?" Even though it was muffled, Eibhleann knew exactly who the voice belonged to.
"She is still sleeping but she stays awake more and more every day," the ladies maid replied. When she heard them speak more, Eibhleann slowly got out of bed and tiptoed closer to the

door to hear better. She and Reid had talked very little ever since she was rescued. Nothing had been said about the situation other than discussing their return home. They hardly saw each other during her recovery at the hotel. She knew they would soon board a ship for home. Things would surely change then. For this, she was a bit nervous. They would surely have plenty of time on their hands and would inevitably talk sooner or later. They were no more than foreigners to one another. Nearly every time she and Reid had seen each other in the last year, it consisted primarily of quarreling. What they once shared seemed far too distant to be real anymore. What made it all the more so was now that Reid was a changed man.

Because of her uneasiness at the thought of spending more time with him, Eibhleann wanted to somehow make sense of his odd behavior. She had to figure her husband out. However, with her recovery taking longer than expected, she hadn't gotten any opportunities.

She slowly neared the door and put her ear up to it.

"What are you going to do?" Eibhleann heard a man's voice now but she couldn't place it.

"I don't have all the answers but I certainly know one thing. I won't make the same mistake this time," Reid answered.

"What mistake?" the person he spoke to asked.

Mistake? New questions instantly arose in Eibhleann. *I shouldn't be listening to this,* she told herself but she wouldn't have stopped for anything. *Yet what is he talking about?* Instead, she endeavored to hear all the more.

"The mistake of trying to fix everything on my own...trying to change my wife. I'm afraid to say I didn't realize it until it was too late. My eyes were forced open to the fact that without God, I could do nothing. I've made a vow to change myself and let God take care of it and work through me in His timing. I'm not going to push her like last time," Reid explained solemnly.

Eibhleann was at a complete loss. Any grasp she thought she had on things vanished. At first she had been skeptical of his self-pronounced change, but his selfless actions at the factory and what he'd just said, made it clear that it was no farce. It was all true. Eibhleann was now growing more apprehensive than ever. Her thoughts and feelings were anything but normal. She was unsure of everything and her emotions out of control.

She had been so overwhelmed, she didn't hear any more of their conversation. Eibhleann wasn't brought back to the present until she heard footsteps coming closer to the door. She gasped and hurried back to her bed, almost tripping in the process.

Eli left after they talked briefly. Reid was also going to leave the hall since he was told his wife was still sleeping. His reason for coming in the first place was to check in on her but since the ladies maid already had, he didn't want to disturb her.

He took a step to leave but hesitated.

What if she has awakened by now? He glanced back at the door to Eibhleann's room. How he wanted to talk to her. Reid longed to have casual conversation like they used to. He was overjoyed that his wife was alive and safe, howbeit, she wasn't truly back as of yet. Eibhleann was distant towards him as though they were still miles apart. Although, they hadn't gotten very many chances to speak during her recovery, the times they did, were strained.

Reid slowly made his way back to the door and raised his hand to knock softly and listen for a reply of some kind, showing him she was awake but abruptly stopped.

Wait. What am I doing? What did I just get through telling Eli? Lord, I promised You that I wouldn't interfere and try to make things happen the way I think they should. Reid was used to having everything figured out but it wasn't the case this time. One minute he wanted to ask Eibhleann about the details of what had taken place since she left Ireland, and then the next moment, he thought it better not to know anything. *Alright...I know it will take time. I will not push her!* he sternly told himself and forced himself to pull his hand away from the door. It would take time to get to know each other again. In many ways, it would be like getting reacquainted anew. His faith was his only anchor. It was the unshakable truth that would bring him through.

Eibhleann heard the footsteps now leave down the hall. She was completely confounded. While she should have felt releaved that Reid decided not to disturb her, she found herself regretting that he hadn't. She slowly sat up in her bed, her eyes filled with tears.

What's wrong with me? she asked herself and held her head in her hands. She felt ashamed, nervous, lonely, embarrassed, and happy to be rescued, all at the same time. *I can't make sense of anything!*

Two more weeks had passed before Reid decided to face his discomfort head on and seek out his wife. He left his cabin and walked out onto the deck. A welcoming breeze met him as he strolled across the deck once he spotted Eibhleann's ladies maid. He could be certain that where the ladies maid was, he could find Eibhleann there as well.

It turned out that she was bringing his wife a tray with scones and tea. There was a small table set up by the rail on the starboard side. It was a nice spot out of the way and the sails provided them some shade. Reid quietly approached.

"Hello," he said when Eibhleann glanced up at him.

"'ello," she replied shyly. Her ladies maid silently took her leave so they could be alone.

"May I?" Reid pulled out the chair across from Eibhleann.

"Yes, t'be sure." After he was seated, she poured him a cup of tea. Reid could tell she was just as aflutter and ill at ease as he.

"How are you feeling?"

"Better every day…an' glad ter be 'eadin' 'ome." She met his gaze, trying to gage his thoughts. Part of her still couldn't believe he would take her back after everything. Deep down she hoped he wasn't merely waiting to return to Ireland before revealing his true motive concerning her. All the unknown questions caused her uneasiness to grow. She wanted to ask but was almost afraid to.

Surely I'll know more as time goes on, Eibhleann tried to calm herself.

"I'm glad to be going home as well…mostly because you'll be with me." His comment caused her to blush slightly. It was the affectionate way he'd said it in a quiet tone. It made her regret her foolish actions all the more. How she wished she could go back and do things differently.

All this time I thought he was the fool.

Reid sipped his tea as the silence wore on, other than the sounds of the sailors hard at work around them. More than anything, Reid wanted to show her how much he still cared for her. The only way he knew how was in his every action and word. On the other hand, he didn't want to go too far. Reid had yet to find the right balance, for patience had never been a strong attribute in him.

"Well, I'll let you get back to your afternoon," he soon finished and stood. Eibhleann nodded in return. In truth, Reid could have stayed there with her forever but he told himself many times that he must not force things. He let things move on naturally with patience.

I'll see her again at supper, he assured himself. It was even more difficult since he really had nothing else to do on the ship. *This journey is surely going to seem long,* he thought, although deep down he presumed the time would do their relationship a lot of good.

CHAPTER TWENTY-SEVEN

August 1816

After their plates were taken from them, Reid and Eibhleann were now alone. The captain and his four officers had eaten dinner with them in the fancy dining room. One by one they eventually excused themselves to get back to work.

Reid wouldn't have wanted it any other way. He'd hoped they might be alone for a while. They had separate cabins for Eibhleann's health reasons, as the doctor had admonished. Reid had a sneaking suspicion that she felt the same since she hadn't made a move to leave as of yet. Besides, they had little else to do.

"Did you hear the captain say we're a bit more than halfway home?" Reid broke the silence.

"Aye, that I did. I'm pure 'appy to hear it. It seems the cabin is growin' smaller every day," Eibhleann said. Reid smiled with how comfortable she was getting around him again. "Why are ya smilin'?" She had caught onto his features and asked. She couldn't help but smile herself.

"Nothing. My cabin feels the same." They both fell quiet once again as they tried to find something to talk about. Reid opened his mouth to say something when Eibhleann glanced up from the table and spoke, this time her tone was more serious.

"Why did ya say those things…back at the factory? I mean…." she stumbled to find the right words. Reid instantly met her gaze at the abrupt mentioning of the factory. This was the first time either of them had spoken of it, or any previous happenings for that matter. He was beginning to wonder if she would ever bring it up.

"What exactly are you referring to?" he asked. Eibhleann felt her face grow warm. She had been too ashamed to ask before but she couldn't hold it back any longer. She had to know.

"Why…." her breath caught in her throat but she forced herself to continue. There was no turning back now. "Why were ya gonna give yer life for mine?" There, it was finally said. Eibhleann lowered her gaze to her lap in embarrassment.

"Because I love you," Reid answered as if it was the simplest of questions. Eibhleann glanced back up at him and in her shock.

How can he love me…after how I've acted? She did all she could to hold back her tears. *No one would give up their life for someone…especially someone who has done the terrible things I have. How can he still love me?*

Reid saw her struggling and decided to go on, but very carefully.

"Eibhleann, God has given me a love for you. A love so great, I would willingly give up my life for you a hundred times over."

"How?" she choked.

"Because I've been shown the greatest love of all…a love

that's not dependent on the other person. There is One who gave His life for us all, regardless of anything we have done," Reid continued. Eibhleann recalled when he had told her of his conversion. It was easy to say those things when he wasn't in danger, but doing it in the midst of trouble showed that what Reid believed was real.

CHAPTER TWENTY-EIGHT

September 1816

The sun was just setting below the waves as Reid walked Eibhleann across the deck and to the hull. "What a fine evening for a walk," Reid stated as they took in the beautiful sky filled with warm hues of orange and red. The enchanting color reflected off of the calm water, making it all the more radiant.

"Aye."

"We've been very fortunate to have this calm weather during our journey," Reid pointed out.

"The captain seems ter think the red clouds are warnin' us of troublesome weather comin'. Do ya think he's correct?" Eibhleann asked.

"I dare say he has more experience than I, yet I hope he's mistaken. I tell myself it's only a lovely sunset," Reid replied just as they reached the opening to the hull. Eibhleann gently pulled her arm from his but before turning to go, Reid grasped her hand. "Thank you for walking with me."

"You're failte," she took in his loving gaze and felt aflutter in her stomach. It was as if they were courting all over again. They stood there for several moments. It wasn't awkward anymore as it had been weeks before.

Eibhleann searched his eyes, trying to read his thoughts. There was hope and an assurance in Reid that she longed for.

"What is it?" he finally asked in a whisper.

"You are truly different." She was almost relieved when he didn't say anything but only smiled slightly. "Do ya think…." *Oh, this was a bad idea!* Eibhleann tried to speak. *You have no right to ask such a thing…especially of him.* Her thoughts flooded over her. "Wud it be possible," she struggled to share her heart yet her doubts were too great and overpowered any glimmer of hope. *You already know the answer! Why even ask? It's impossible to have what he has.*

"Do I think what? It's alright," Reid tried to help her.

"Oh, it's nothin'." Eibhleann started to pull away from him.

"You're sure?"

"Aye…please, jist never mind," Eibhleann sighed.

"Are you alright?" he asked.

"I'm grand. Goodnight." With that, she made her way into the hull and to her cabin.

Once she closed the door and was alone, she glanced up at the ceiling and leaning back against the door. Bitter tears of regret crept swiftly down her cheeks.

"I'm such a fool…I can never be forgiven."

Eibhleann tried to tell herself it was no use to ever think of obtaining forgiveness for her past. The hopeless feeling didn't go away but lingered into the day. She did her best to appear normal and indifferent in front of Reid yet she could tell he was concerned about her, although he said nothing.

When evening came she still couldn't push it aside completely. Eibhleann couldn't go on any longer like this. She had to ask. She had to make herself talk to Reid. At supper, she went back and forth within herself, waiting for the right time to speak to him. However, when the opportunity presented itself and her and Reid had arrived at the dining room at the same time before everyone else, Eibhleann's shame wouldn't allow her to go through with it. Her guilt was so strong she couldn't bring it up.

By the time the captain and his officers arrived and the food was served, Eibhleann was too distressed to eat a bite. Time wore on and she was only growing more upset with herself. Reid and the other men were in deep conversation when an idea suddenly struck her. She even gasped when it came to her. The men immediately stopped talking and glanced at her, causing her to blush.

"Everything alright?" Reid asked quietly, directly across the table from her.

"Aye…um…please excuse me," she nervously stood to her feet, set her napkin on the table and bustled out of the room. Eibhleann rushed to her cabin and to the small nightstand. She swiftly pulled the top drawer open and rustled through it.

Oh, where did I put…there it is! Eibhleann held up a small writing tablet in triumph.

Only minutes later, when she finished writing, she folded the note.

"Now just to deliver it," she mumbled to herself. She had to be quick about it while Reid was still in the dining room. The way she abruptly left was bound to concern her husband. *He might come looking for me,* she thought and went for the door.

Once at Reid's cabin, Eibhleann apprehensively turned the doorknob and opened it a little. She took one last glance down the hall then slipped inside. She simply set the envelope on top of his bed and left.

It wasn't until hours later that Reid walked to his small bunk and saw something lying on top of the blanket. He reached for the candle beside the bed and lit it. Reid held it up then quickly sat down to open the note.

Dear Reid,

You are a different person than you used to be. I want what you have but I don't know if I can be forgiven. I don't have the right words to ask you.

Eibhleann

Reid finished reading then wiped his eyes. How he had dreamed of Eibhleann saying these very words. He had never been happier.

"Lord, please show me what to say…so that she can accept it and understand," he prayed, his voice filled with emotion. His first impulse was to go to Eibhleann straight away yet he couldn't be too quick about it. He had to wait until he had the right words to say. He wanted to be led.

He barely slept a wink by the time morning came as he continued to pray for guidance. Dawn couldn't have come soon enough. Reid quickly dressed and left to deliver his joyous reply. Because it was so early, he stepped up to Eibhleann's cabin as quietly as possible and slid the note under the door. He didn't notice until returning to his own room that the hall was a bit tipsy from rough waves.

I hope the captain wasn't right about bad weather coming. It's beginning to feel like he might be. Reid slowed his pace and very carefully made his way back to his cabin.

Eibhleann awoke when she heard something fall to the floor with a loud crash. She sat up and saw that the wash basin had fallen off the dresser.

Oh no…is it indeed a storm? she asked herself as she got up from her bunk to clean the mess. Thankfully, the basin wasn't broken. It merely slipped off the dresser. Eibhleann reached for a towel to dry the floor when something caught her eye by the door. She turned to see what it was and saw an envelope.

Reid must have put it under the door! She immediately forgot about cleaning up and went to the note, opening it in haste.

Dear Eibhleann,

You can be forgiven. There is nothing you could do to change that. There is none righteous, no, not one. All you must do is ask God to forgive you and accept Jesus as your Lord and Savior. When you put your trust in Him, He takes all of the sin onto Himself. He did this when He died on the cross. He gave His life for you and I. It is a free gift you only have to accept. If you will do this, I assure you, you will gain the freedom you seek.

Affectionately yours,

Reid

Eibhleann thought deeply on everything she had read. However, it wasn't long before a new string of doubts traipsed in.

That's it? This is all it takes to be forgiven? Surely it's not this simple. She didn't have much more time to muse for at that moment she quickly reached out to brace herself as her cabin swayed to the right, then to the left. In a way, it was almost worse not having a single window to look out of to see just how high the violent waves were.

CHAPTER TWENTY-NINE

The captain was correct. A storm overtook their vessel. For nearly three days and three nights the ship was tossed about. Both Reid and Eibhleann were admonished to stay safely inside their cabins. Someone would then bring their meals to them, although neither one of them wished for much food while minor seasickness had befallen them. The only consolation was, the captain said the storm was actually carrying them toward their wanted destination. They would hopefully reach land soon.

Not being able to talk to Eibhleann made it seem like forever to Reid before the weather began to calm. Finally, the storm passed during the third night. When everyone awoke the next morning, they all shared in the relief.

Reid and Eibhleann happily made their way to the dining room to eat their first full meal in days. That, and not being able to see one another made their steps a little lighter and faster.

"Good morning, Eibhleann," Reid greeted the moment he entered.

"Good mornin' to ya," she answered and took a seat. Reid couldn't help but stare at her, trying to see any sign of newfound hope. He soon realized it to be difficult to read her thoughts. He dearly hoped she would reveal good news as soon as they had a chance to be alone.

"How did you do through the storm?"

"Quite nauseous really. I'm pure glad it's over. How aboyt yer?" Eibhleann asked him.

"About the same. It was worse not being able to see you," Reid said and was relieved to see her smile.

The captain and his officers were finally seated before the meal began.

As the morning went on, Eibhleann never mentioned anything about Reid's note, nor hers. She acted as if nothing of the sort had even taken place. Reid didn't know what to think. He didn't want to push her, yet he wanted to know so badly. He hoped she understood his letter but how could he know for sure if she said nothing?

After lunch they went their separate ways until later that afternoon. Reid was roaming around on deck when he spotted Eibhleann sitting alone at the stern. It was a secluded spot at the very end of the ship. She was gazing over the sea.

Maybe she doesn't want to be disturbed, he thought. Yet something in him urged him to at least find out. "May I join you?" he quietly asked so not to startle her. Eibhleann looked at him and nodded. Reid walked over to where she sat. He lowered to sit down next to her hesitantly. He looked at her closely but alas, her features were still a mystery to him. *Lord, what should I do? Should I ask her about the note?* Reid silently prayed. Eibhleann returned her gaze over the rail. It seemed like they both wanted to say something yet neither could bring themselves to. In that silence, Reid got his answer. He now knew what to do.

"May I tell you about something that took place when you left Ireland?" he broke the unwieldy silence.

"Gran' so."

"I uh…." he cleared his throat, trying to share his heart and put it into the right words. "After I hurried to our place on the coast and found the necklace…and it hit me that you had perished…I had never been so disheartened." Though Reid didn't look at Eibhleann as he spoke, his peripheral vision showed the guilt that washed over her. "I was sorrowful over one thing above all else. I was so afraid because you had never come to accept your salvation…the very thing that decides your eternity. I couldn't bring myself to the fact that I would never see you again, in this life or the next. I truly came to the end of myself that day. I realized I couldn't save you. I failed to lead you to the truth because I was trying to do it without God." Reid glanced out over the waves and sighed. He willed himself to go on. He would never forget the sorrow he had felt that day.

He hesitated with emotion before he was able to continue. "When He led me to believe you weren't dead and I found out where you might have gone, I went after you. I swore I would never make that mistake again. I had to let you go when I believed you to be gone forever. I promised God if I did find you alive, I wouldn't stray from my promise. I would only do my part to show you the way. I've held true to it ever since then, as hard as it was at times." Reid moved to face Eibhleann and took her hands in his. "Eibhleann, I love you. I never want to lose you here or in eternity." With that, he opened her hand so she could see that he had placed something in it. The minute she caught sight of it, Eibhleann's breath caught in her throat. She lifted up the necklace in front of her just as a tear rolled down her cheek.

He saved it all this time, she was overcome.

"I hope and pray that you can find it in your heart to forgive me," Reid went on. Eibhleann's gaze shot back to him. He surprised her again by slowly standing to his feet. "I take my leave now to allow you some time alone."

Forgive him? He wants my forgiveness? Me...of all people! Eibhleann could say nothing but only watched him leave. *When I hurt him the most?* She began to cry harder as she continued to hold the necklace. She glanced heavenward and wiped her wet face. How she wanted to pray then and there and know the One who had saved her husband. She yearned to know God as Reid did but she felt so far from Him. She held on to too many things; things that kept her from getting closer to the Lord.

I can't forgive myself much less anyone else. How can I ever come before God? As impossible as she felt it to be, the love that Reid had shown her, which he said came only from God intrigued her. It drew her to it. She had no desire to fight it as she once did. She wanted nothing more than to give up and put her trust in someone greater. Eibhleann opened her mouth to call on Him but only ended up burying her face in her hands.

Eibhleann was awakened in the night. Someone called her name and it startled her. She sat up in the dark room and sighed heavily. The burden she held weighed heavily on her. So much so, her breathing even felt heavy and labored.

Could the voice be Him? she asked herself. She was indeed alone in her cabin. Eibhleann knew she couldn't do this anymore. Something had to change. She would do anything to change it. Without waiting one more second, she got out of bed and knelt beside it.

"God...." The moment she said His name, she began to weep. "I can't do this...I nade Yer. Even though I don't understan', please help me. Please forgive me for everythin' I've done," her voice wavered, "I'm so sorry. I take You now as me Savior...and me Lord, amen." There, on her knees, the weight that was so heavy, disappeared. It was gone!

CHAPTER THIRTY

ibhleann tossed and turned, trying to get away from her tortured thoughts. Her past haunted her to no end. For an entire week following her conversion she had felt at peace and carefree but all of a sudden flash backs of everything she had done started to come back. Each memory seemed to scoff at her, telling her she was a fool to think she could just forget them.

"No! No!" Eibhleann placed her hand on her perspiring forehead. "Leave me alone!" she spoke to her mind in desperation but her troubles wouldn't relent. Her unsettling past now washed over her in waves.

What should I do? Eibhleann asked herself. Another thought then came to her, yet it was small compared to all the others that hung over her. *I've asked for God's forgiveness but I haven't spoken a word to the person I've hurt the most.* She threw her blankets aside and nearly jumped out of bed. She reached for a shawl and rushed out of her cabin.

By the time she reached Reid's cabin she was almost in hysterics. Never once did she think of waiting until morning. She was too distraught to wait a moment longer. Eibhleann knocked but no one answered. Instead of pounding on the door again, she opened it with such force that it banged against the wall. It obviously startled Reid for he instantly sat up.

"I'm sorry…I jist," Eibhleann choked.

"Eibhleann?" Reid gasped in shock. "What is wrong?" he swung his feet out of his bunk just as she hastened to him.

"I'm sorry for everythin'!" She was so relieved when Reid welcomed her with open arms. It felt so good to be held by him and Reid in turn thought it felt just as wonderful to hold her. Eibhleann wept in his arms for some time before she could go on.

"I'm sorry for goin' behind your back with so many secrets…an' for makin' you tink you wus dead…for hurtin' ya. I regret it so greatly."

"I forgive you," Reid tried to comfort her. He had forgiven her long ago, although it wasn't easy at first.

Eibhleann eventually pulled away just a little to meet his gaze. His love that she had managed to push away so long ago began to rise up from deep inside her as she looked at Reid. His eyes blazed with affection, more than any love she'd ever known. Everything Eibhleann had felt upon first meeting him was rekindled anew. Although this time she had no hidden motives. She had no intention of merely playing with his heart as she had done in the past and with others as well. The resentment and animosity she saw in life had all but washed away. She hadn't realized it until that moment. All that was left was the sincere and ardent love for him. It was now unhindered by what she could get out of the relationship like she used to measure things by.

How much Reid fervently cared for her began to inundate her. He leaned his forehead onto hers. His grey blue eyes drew Eibhleann in as he passionately kissed her.

"How can yer forgive me as if nathin' 'appened?" she breathed.

"Someone who has been greatly forgiven can forgive greatly," Reid's touch lingered after he very slowly wiped away a tear on Eibhleann's face.

"I prayed to God days ago an' asked Him to save me," she revealed. Reid instantly became more attentive upon hearing this, although he already had his suspicions. "I felt at peace an' carefree but the guilt has cum back. Jist a wee bit at first, then more and more. I asked for God's forgiveness but I can't git away from al' I've done," Eibhleann hung her head in despair.

"It's not enough to know you're forgiven. You must believe in the remission of your sins…that you've been redeemed from sin. Here, I'll show you what I mean," Reid reached under his bunk for his Bible. Eibhleann watched in wonder as he swiftly paged through the well-worn book as if he was well acquainted with its pages. "Here it is," he stopped, "You must read this to understand. Start here."

Upon returning to her cabin, Eibhleann lit a candle then sat on her bed. She set down the Bible on her lap and opened it. She hesitated at first.

How can all the answers be in this book? she tried to grasp it and understand how easily Reid trusted the words. Howbeit, she was desperate to be free. There was nowhere else to turn to. She began to read in the four different places where Reid had instructed.

²³ *For all have sinned, and come short of the glory of God;*

²⁴ *Being justified freely by his grace through the redemption that is in Christ Jesus:*

²⁵ *Whom God hath set forth to be a propitiation through faith in his blood, to declare his righteousness for the remission of sins that are past, through the forbearance of God;*

²⁶ *To declare, I say, at this time his righteousness: that he might be just, and the justifier of him which believeth in Jesus.*

Romans 3:23-26

⁸ *But God commendeth his love toward us, in that, while we were yet sinners, Christ died for us.*

⁹ *Much more then, being now justified by his blood, we shall be saved from wrath through him.*

¹⁰ *For if, when we were enemies, we were reconciled to God by the death of his Son, much more, being reconciled, we shall be saved by his life.*

¹¹ *And not only so, but we also joy in God through our Lord Jesus Christ, by whom we have now received the atonement.*

Romans 5:8-11

17 Therefore if any man be in Christ, he is a new creature: old things are passed away; behold, all things are become new.

18 And all things are of God, who hath reconciled us to himself by Jesus Christ, and hath given to us the ministry of reconciliation;

19 To wit, that God was in Christ, reconciling the world unto himself, not imputing their trespasses unto them; and hath committed unto us the word of reconciliation.

20 Now then we are ambassadors for Christ, as though God did beseech you by us: we pray you in Christ's stead, be ye reconciled to God.

21 For he hath made him to be sin for us, who knew no sin; that we might be made the righteousness of God in him.

2 Corinthians 5:17-21

7 In whom we have redemption through his blood, the forgiveness of sins, according to the riches of his grace;

Ephesians 1:7

After reading the glorious verses, Eibhleann sighed.
What does it all mean? To be reconciled and justified with God by the death of His Son? I can be saved by His life? It sounds wonderful.

CHAPTER THIRTY-ONE

October 1816

" $\mathcal{E}$ ibhleann, there you are," Reid called to her once she appeared on deck along with her ladies maid. They weaved through the sailors who were busy with unloading the ship.

"Perhaps you should go on to Saerlaith with some of the staff. I will stay with the men to make sure everything is unloaded correctly."

"Alright," Eibhleann could barely contain her delight to get off the ship all the sooner. There was nothing else for her to do aboard so she readily agreed.

Hours later, Reid also anxiously made his way home. Saerlaith was a wonderful sight, especially with Eibhleann being restored to him in many ways.

He made his way through the Great Hall and into another hall when he found Elmira coming to greet him.

"Reid!" she rushed up to give him a hug and to kiss his cheek. "I'm so happy you've returned and with Eibhleann as well! It's surely a miracle."

"Mother, you have no idea. It's nothing but a miracle."

"When she walked through the door, I very nearly fainted in shock," Elmira explained. Reid looked past his mother in search of his wife.

"Where is she anyway?"

"I believe she went to the gardens."

Reid took his leave to search out Eibhleann. On his way to the side entrance onto the veranda that in turn overlooked the gardens, Paul Wilkinson, met him.

"Glad to have ya home, My Lord."

"It's good to be back." The men shook hands, "How has everything been in my absence?"

"Good for the most part. There was one incident."

"More vandalism?" Reid inquired of the steward.

"Unfortunately, yes. One morning Orrin went out to feed the horses and livestock to find out they had been slaughtered…every last one of them," Wilkinson painfully explained. "This same thing happened to one other tenant."

Reid's newfound joy tempted to fall at the sad news.

"Who has done this?" he asked but could only picture one person doing something so hateful.

"Well, that's another thing," Wilkinson lowered his voice and stepped closer to assure he wouldn't be overheard. "We've heard tell that the man who shot you has been seen in the area."

"What?"

"Aye, in the company of your brother, Garrick." It was just as Reid had feared, however, the shock over hearing it told to him was still considerable.

"When? Where?"

"Right after our animals were killed. Though, I don't know where they were seen together."

"Why can't he face me like a man?" Reid said through clenched teeth.

"We've managed to keep it pretty quiet…for your mother's sake. To not upset her," Wilkinson went on.

"Good," he replied but was deep in thought over what to do about it. All he knew was, now was not the time. "Let's talk more about this later. Thank you."

"Certainly, My Lord."

"Welcome home, My Lord."

"Thank you, Mr. McCline. It's good to be home. Have you seen Lady Kerrich?" Reid asked the head gardener.

"Aye, she asked for a horse then rode that way." Reid followed the direction the gardener was pointing in and smiled.

"Thank you," he quickly left.

After obtaining a horse he rode to the well-known place on the coast. As he neared it, Reid heard something on the wind. It was like heaven to his ears as he came upon Eibhleann. She was facing the sea and was singing a beautiful tune. He had never heard it before. She sang in Gaelic so he couldn't understand the words. He couldn't dismount just yet as he took in her voice.

"Tar, thou fount de gach beannacht,

tune mo chroí a chanadh dod ghrásta;

sruthanna na trócaire, riamh scor,

glaoch ar amhráin de moladh loudest.

Múin dom roinnt sonnet melodious,

chanadh ag dteangacha flaming thuas."

It was like nothing he'd ever heard before, especially from her. The passion in her voice clearly proclaimed that the words moved her deeply. It was then that Eibhleann turned to Reid. She didn't stop singing though. Instead, she changed over to English.

"Praise the mount! I'm fixed upon it,

mount of thy redeemin' love."

She smiled adoringly at Reid as he slowly dismounted. The words made the song all the more inspiring for it was about their beloved Savior. They both covered the distance between them. Reid instantly saw the difference in her appearance he'd never witnessed before. A great joy was upon her and it poured through her bright eyes. A light seemed to envelop her. She was truly free from the lingering doubts that had hung over her for so long.

"Jesus sought me when a stranger,

wanderin' from the fold of God;

He, to rescue me from danger,

interposed His precious blood."

Eibhleann finished the song when they reached one another.

"You look like a new person," Reid spoke softly. Eibhleann nodded, tears glistened on her face in the sunlight.

"I am. After readin' those verses…I wus confused at first. Then today, a light came ter me. I nigh nu what ya mean…aboyt knowin' I'm redeemed and free from sin. I'm free at last!" she exclaimed. Reid drew her to him in an embrace then lowered to kiss her tenderly.

PART III

CHAPTER THIRTY-TWO

March 1821

" $\mathcal{E}$ ibhleann, turned over and placed her hand on Reid's side of the bed only to find it empty. When she slowly opened her eyes and saw he was indeed gone, she moved her gaze to the bed stand.

His Bible is gone, she yawned as she sat up to figure out the time. *Not even dawn.* By now she was too alert to go back to sleep. Instead of lying back down against her pillow, Eibhleann got out of bed. She immediately caught sight of a light outside her window, for the sky was still somewhat dark. She went to the window to see where the light was coming from and smiled.

"I thought that wus your light I saw." Reid looked up to see Eibhleann walking towards him from the house.

"I didn't wake you, I hope."

"Not at al'," she bent over and kissed his cheek before moving to the chair beside him on the veranda. "Chucker yer mind if I sit or wud ya rather be alone?" she asked when she spotted the open Bible on Reid's lap.

"That would be fine. I was about done," Reid replied.

"Troubled aboyt yer brother again?" she asked. Reid nodded.

"I've been praying…asking God what I should do about him. No one knows where he is, yet the attacks are growing worse. I know he's behind them…maybe not all but most. The last time Garrick was seen, was right before we returned when all of our animals were killed. Our tenants are being tormented nearly every week. Fires, animals being slaughtered, supplies stolen. Just yesterday, McCarthy was stopped on the road. He was beaten in front of his family, everything in their wagon was taken, then they finished up by violently killing their only horse. It's becoming unsafe to go anywhere and I'm weary of it. I don't want to live in fear…and now with you being in the family way…it weighs heavily on my mind," Reid ended his frustrated rant by taking Eibhleann's hand and sighing.

"Don't worry…especially on my account."

"I just don't want anything to happen to you. I couldn't bare—" Eibhleann raised her hand to Reid's lips.

"Ya alwus tell me to trust God an' the importance av givin' your cares ter Him. Don't take them back nigh."

"You're right," Reid admitted.

For the next few moments they sat in silence, hand in hand, looking out over the view. It was slowly getting lighter and the fog drifted along the coast. All of a sudden Eibhleann gasped.

"What? What's wrong?" Reid jumped and quickly leaned forward.

"Nothin' silly. The babe is movin' is al'," she chuckled and placed Reid's hand over her belly.

Dawn was upon them when something interrupted the quiet. Two men on horses rode up to the house in a hurry.

"Go and get some men up. I'll get Lord Kerrich." Because it was so still, Reid and Eibhleann could hear what they were saying. The man, who had spoken, came up to the veranda and quickly got off his steed in his haste then marched to the door of the house. On his way however, he caught a glimpse of Reid and Eibhleann for the first time.

"Oh, Lord Kerrich, you're awake. Good."

"Eli, what is it?" Reid immediately stood when he heard the anxiety in his land steward's voice. Eli had been promoted from footman to the land steward shortly after their return to Ireland. He had taken the place of the previous steward, Roland Carver.

"You're brother, we've found him."

"Where is he?"

"Not far from here. He and a handful of men are camped out right on the edge of our land," Eli solemnly explained. Reid exchanged a swift glance with Eibhleann in apprehension.

"Mind yerself," Eibhleann urged.

"I will. I'll put a stop to this today." The vengeful tone in Reid's voice did nothing to ease her.

CHAPTER THIRTY-THREE

hat should I say? What will he do when we meet? Countless conflicting thoughts flashed through Reid's mind as he and his men silently rode to the place where Garrick had been spotted. On the way, Eli informed him that Garrick and the men with him were still asleep when they had been found.

Eli gave the signal that they were nearing the place so they all dismounted to sneak up on them on foot. Questions still bombarded Reid's mind as he crept up to the place as quietly as he could. Sure enough, Garrick was asleep on the ground along with four other men. Reid stopped and crouched behind a tree to get a better look at them, his men close behind. He glanced at each of the other men to see if he knew any of them when his gaze suddenly stopped on the last man.

"What is it?" Eli whispered when Reid's breath caught in his throat.

"The man who shot me...that's him."

"You're certain?"

"I'm more sure than anything." Reid was instantly brought back to that horrible night when he faced the man he'd never seen before. He could still picture the strange look on his face and the smile that slowly formed as he pulled the gun out. Reid's eyes shut and he flinched as the sound of the gun seemed to echo in his ears. He'd always wondered if Garrick had been behind that as well. He had hoped it wasn't true.

But it is true. All of it. I now know he has been behind every attack. A cold sweat came over him as he relived every hateful thing his brother had done the last few years, not to mention the pain Reid had endured.

Reid finally stood up straight with clenched fists in rage. From somewhere outside himself, it felt like something came over him and nearly took over, leaving Reid off to the side to watch.

"Surround them and only do as I say," he ordered solemnly and started walking toward the sleeping men.

"What's he goin' to do?" Reid overheard one of his newer footman ask another fellow staff.

"Dunno really...probably end it here and now to finally rid 'imself of the man who shot him and maybe his brother," the other man whispered in return, "At least that's what I would do. Forget the law and take care of them meself."

"Aye, I would do the same. Can't blame him." What the two footmen suggested slowly dawned on Reid as he continued on.

Perhaps they're right. Who could blame me if I took matters into my own hands? If it were the other way around, that man would surely kill me if given the chance all over again. The thought started out small but it grew with every step he took. Reid's anger was becoming so great he couldn't reason correctly anymore. Memories of how he'd suffered consumed his thoughts.

Without realizing it, he pulled the gun from his belt by the time he stood over his brother. Reid reached for Garrick's gun that was sitting beside him and threw it out of reach. He no longer cared if they heard him and woke up. He was about to call out his brother's name and raise his pistol when his arm wouldn't move. It felt weighed down by some unseen force. He glanced down at his hand to see what was going on. Reid tried several times more but his hand wouldn't budge. He eventually moved his gaze to Garrick, who still lay unmoving. By now some of the fight in Reid had waned. He then glanced at the man who had shot him.

What am I doing? How can I do this? What will revenge like this accomplish? His conscience rose up once his fury made room for it. He now knew it was no strange coincidence that he was stopped but it was divine intervention.

I could do far more with this chance. It might be the only time I can talk to him…to reason with him and finally get his attention. Instead of recalling past miseries, Reid began to remember the great mercy and forgiveness shown to him. *When I didn't deserve it,* he thought as his anger vanished. In its place aroused the importance to take advantage of the moment.

Reid looked up from the sleeping men and saw his own men in place and armed, ready for his word to act. *This is it. I have nothing to lose.* Wisdom and direction washed over him, much like the rage did earlier. Reid stooped down and lifted Garrick's hand. His brother had always been a hard sleeper so Reid wasn't surprised that he didn't stir as he slipped the large ring off of his finger. Garrick's father had given him the ring when he was just a boy before he died in the war. He had worn it ever since he'd grown into it.

Reid took a deep breath as he backed away from the middle of the camp. He then raised his gun over his head and fired it. All the men startled awake and instantly got up to reach for their weapons.

"Move slowly for you're surrounded!" Reid shouted before they could reach for their guns. They glanced around helplessly, confused and disorientated. "Brother." Hearing Reid call out to him made Garrick spin around to finally see him. He tried to appear calm at the sight of him, but in truth, he was now more fearful than ever because he had been caught so close to Saerlaith.

"Reid…I—" Garrick began to speak but was interrupted.

"By your own eyes, you are a witness to how the Lord has delivered you into my hand," Reid shouted with assurance.

"The Lord?" Garrick scoffed but it didn't sway Reid in the least. He continued and glanced at the man who had tried to kill him.

"Some of my men bade me to kill you…." Garrick stiffened at Reid's statement. "But I will spare you."

"Why?"

"To show you that I mean no harm or evil toward you. I never have…yet you continually harass me, my tenants, and my land. I still don't understand why. What have I done to you to deserve this? What are you even doing here?" Reid didn't give his brother a chance to explain for he knew he wouldn't anyway. "I want to warn you. Because I didn't sin against you today, the Lord will avenge me if you don't stop these hateful acts."

"So, what are you going to do?" Garrick gazed down at the ground. He detested not having the control of the situation.

"What I've always wanted to do. I want to treat you as my brother, not my enemy," Reid answered. Garrick glanced back up at this in surprise. "I want us to work together…I want to share what has been given to me."

Garrick was trying to make sense of what he'd just heard. He couldn't grasp what Reid was saying. His brother wanting to treat him kindly instead of revenge was completely foreign to him, especially after all he'd done.

Reid looked steadily on Garrick to see what he would do. He could tell Garrick was trying to understand. Reid then threw the ring he held to his brother to prove what he said was true. Garrick's life had indeed been in Reid's hands but was spared. After he caught it and saw it was his ring, he could only stare at it for some time. For a brief moment, it looked as though Garrick's guard was softening. Reid silently prayed he would see reason.

Everyone was at a standstill until Garrick tightened his grip on the ring and he met Reid's gaze.

"You should have killed me when you had the chance," he sneered through clenched teeth. "You're a fool just like everyone knows you to be. Let's go!" Garrick turned to his men.

Reid sadly watched them quickly go for their horses. He could tell his own men that were scattered around, were anxiously waiting for him to give some kind of order to act, but he never did.

"You'll be sorry!" Garrick spitefully shouted back as they rode away.

CHAPTER THIRTY-FOUR

June 1821

 o ya 'av a name in mind yet?" Eibhleann looked across the table at Reid and smiled at her mother's question. "We 'av a few in mind," she replied secretively.

"I dare say, that's al' she's gonna say aboyt it," Liam, Eibhleann's father put in just as there was a knock at the door. The foursome thought it strange when the door opened a little and Saerlaith's driver peeked his head in.

"I'm sorry to interrupt, My Lord. There appears to be trouble comin'." Reid instantly stood and went to the window. The sun had set and it was growing dark. Thunder clouds were slowly moving across the sky. Reid saw four men riding toward his in-laws small house. Fear rose up in him as he recalled Garrick's threatening words the last time he'd seen him. He knew it could be no one else.

"What is it?" Eibhleann questioned.

"My brother," Reid turned away from the window. "Deirdre, please take Eibhleann with you into the bedroom as a precaution," he instructed somberly. The two women obeyed at once. Reid's main concern was Eibhleann's safetly and their unborn child.

Donald, the driver, entered and shut the door behind him. They then went about to close the shutters over the windows as Liam went for his shot gun. They soon heard the horses approach, followed by laughing.

It's undoubtingly Garrick...he must be full of spirits, Reid anxiously thought. He opened one of the shutters slightly to see Garrick climb off his horse and stagger closer. He and the three men with him were holding torches. *Oh no,* Reid's heart plummeted into his stomach when he realized what they were up to.

"Best ter stay inside," Liam said when Reid moved to the door. "We can bar the door."

"I have to go out and face him." *It's the only way,* Reid gulped and reached for the door handle. "Lord, deliver us," he prayed under his breath and opened it.

"Garrick, what do you want?" Reid shut the door behind him. The men were hollering and jeering on so Reid had to shout above them. Garrick met his stern gaze.

"Well, brother…." he chuckled, "You said you wanted to see more of me…so here I am!" he started to laugh harder with the others. He couldn't stand still and nearly stumbled.

"You're full of spirits. Go home and leave us be." This made Garrick serious up a bit. It also angered him with being told what to do.

"Oh, I will…just as soon as I finish this." Garrick's men

started up their snickering again as he stepped forward and held the torch toward the house.

"You'll do no such thing here!" This only brought on more scoffing and bellowing.

"Oh yeah? And who's going to stop me?"

"God is my shield and my fortress. What can man do to me? My enemy shall come to me one way and flee before me seven ways." Instead of allowing fear to sway him, courage rose up in Reid. "In the Name of Jesus, you will not hurt me or bring harm to this house!" A flash of lightening, along with a crash of thunder sounded just as the last word left his mouth. This made the men flinch. It even surprised Reid a bit.

Garrick stood still for a moment but then went through with his cruel intention by thrusting the torch onto the house. To everyone's amazement, when it touched the thatched roof, the fire went out. This didn't stop Garrick. He refused to give up. He ran up to one of his men, ripped the torch out of his hand, then did the same. However, it went out as if he had submerged the fire into a bucket of water.

Another roll of thunder echoed loudly.

"Let's get out of here!" one of Garrick's men slowly backed away from the house in disbelief. He quickly went to his horse and climbed onto it. Garrick quietly stepped toward his horse as well. Before he mounted, he took another torch from his last remaining man walking and threw it into the only window that wasn't covered by a shudder.

Reid watched them leave then hurried back inside. He was relieved to find Liam holding the unlit torch and standing among broken glass.

"Everyone alright in here?" Reid breathed.

"Yes, merely a banjacked window. I don't understand! We saw the whole thing! By the time the last torch came through the window, the fire 'ad gone out." As Liam spoke in wonder,

Eibhleann opened the door to the bedroom then her and her mother came out.

"Thank God you're safe!" Eibhleann rushed to Reid and kissed him.

"Thank God indeed…it was the Lord's doing!" Reid tried to come to terms with what had happened. "He has saved us!"

CHAPTER THIRTY-FIVE

September 1821

" ord Kerrich, gran' to see ya."

"And you as well. I had to come out and see how the addition is coming along." Mr. Whelan approached and took the reins from Reid after he dismounted.

"I 'ear ya have a new addition yerself. Congratulations." The men shook hands.

"That we do. He's nearly a month old now."

"And what is the young master's name?" Mrs. Whelan overheard their conversation and came closer.

"Rylan Marden Lennox."

"A gran' name so'tiz. And yar wife is farin' well?"

"Yes, very well. So let us have a look at your growing house," Reid glanced at the home behind the couple.

"Aye, it's much needed for a growin' family," Mr. Whelan chuckled as he tied Reid's horse to a shoddy fence and led the way to their building in progress.

"It certainly is coming along quickly."

"Thanks to the 'elp you supplied."

"I just wanted to make sure it would be finished before winter," Reid explained as they walked along the side of the house. Several children were playing in the yard.

"Has there been trouble of any kind?" he asked and grew serious.

"Naw, we've been pure fortunate. Word got raun aboyt what 'appened with you earlier this summer."

"I'm sure it has."

"'av ya seen or heard from the paddy since?" Mrs. Whelan asked.

"No…nothing."

"Ya don't soun' relieved by it," she pointed out.

"While I am hoping that was the end of the attacks, I can't help but wonder if nothing is good or not. It almost makes me more troubled not knowing where he is," Reid explained.

"Aye, I see what ya mean." All of a sudden, a gunshot was heard. Reid and Mr. Whelan spun around to see where it had come from.

"Garrick…." Reid sighed as soon as his gaze fell upon his brother.

"Children, inside!" Mrs. Whelan quickly gathered her frightened children and ushered them inside the house.

"I'll go and get my—"

"No, I'll take care of this," Reid told Mr. Whelan, "You go inside with your family."

"Are ya—"

"Please," he urged.

"Alright…stay safe." Mr. Whelan finally left.

Reid took a deep breath and apprehensively met his brother head on as he came riding over.

"Garrick, I haven't seen you in months," he greeted and remained guarded for he didn't know what Garrick was planning.

"I'm disappointed you didn't tell me of the good news yourself," Though he wasn't drunk at the time, Garrick's tone sounded as if he wanted to provoke him somehow. "Instead I had to find out about it from someone else." Reid didn't know how to respond much less try to figure out what he was up to.

Why does he care about my son when he attempted to harm us only months ago? "What do you want?" Reid asked sternly. He was done playing this game. Garrick however, wasn't finished yet.

"Well, don't worry over keeping it from me. I made things right and paid them a visit myself," he taunted as he got off his horse and took a step closer. He clearly enjoyed watching Reid stiffen in fear.

"What?"

"You heard me."

"What did you do?" Alarm washed over him when a wicked smile formed of Garrick's face.

"Your wife is a pretty thing. It's a shame she's Irish," Garrick kept coming closer until he was face to face with Reid. "Your son looks much like her."

"What did you do? Tell me!" Reid's voice grew in volume along with his alarm.

"Not much like you though…interesting if you ask me." He still wore the dark grin. It was too much for Reid. He abruptly grabbed ahold of Garrick's collar.

"Tell me what you've done!" he demanded through gritted teeth. Garrick only sneered in return and roughly pushed his grip away. Panic grew in Reid, so much so, he couldn't stay and deal with his cruel brother any longer. He had to get to his wife and son!

Reid instantly turned to run to his steed. Once there, he hurriedly placed his foot in the stirrup and began to lift himself up onto the saddle when Garrick rushed up behind him. He snatched the back of his coat and pulled Reid to the ground.

"Stop it!" Reid tried to get up but was kicked down. He swiftly got up once again, this time ready to defend himself. Garrick attempted to throw his fist at him but Reid managed to jerk to the side and missed the blow. As Garrick stepped forward, Reid shoved him over for he was between him and his horse. Garrick caught his footing too soon and moved in his way. He then pulled out a dagger.

"You don't want to do this!" Reid huffed and put his hands out toward him. The same evil grin appeared on Garrick's face as he suddenly lunged toward Reid over and over, waving the knife. Reid had little choice but to move back to keep from getting cut. He couldn't believe this was his brother attacking him. Garrick was truly estranged to him and very much his enemy.

Garrick somehow jumped forward and was nearly upon him. Reid put his arm up to shield himself as his brother drove the dagger sideways. It slashed his forearm, causing Reid to cry out in pain. Garrick was going to thrust him again when adrenaline set in from being hurt. Reid rose up and punched his brother in the face with his other fist with such force, it sent him falling backwards. Reid took this split second chance to stumble toward his horse. He rode away before Garrick could get to his feet and reach him.

He was still miles away from Saerlaith when he spotted smoke in the sky.

"God help us! Deliver us as You have in times past!" Reid pushed his horse onward as hard as he could to get there speedily.

The staff was already at work trying to put out and contain the fire that set ablaze the west wing of the estate. Reid jumped off his steed and sought out the butler.

"My Lord! The fire…it started moments ago!" Hughes stuttered in his distressed state. He was nearly black with soot and smoke from helping.

"Never mind all of that. Is everyone out of the house?" Reid asked.

"Yes, yes…." Though his answer was positive, he was quite overwhelmed and his face told Reid otherwise. He ultimately grasped the short man by the shoulders to get a direct answer.

"Is anyone still in the house?" Reid asked again, this time more slowly and in all seriousness.

"No…everyone is out…I'm sure of it."

"Alright," Reid finally released him, "We must get the men—"

"My Lord, your arm! What happened?" Hughes noticed the blood seeping through Reid's white shirt.

"It doesn't matter right now. We must organize the men to put a stop to this!"

Reid helped along with everyone else, throwing pail after pail of water onto the flames. Unfortunately, they weren't making much progress. Any other landlord would readily obtain help from neighboring estates to fight the fire, but not Saerlaith. Reid knew all too well they were alone in this for he and his family were hated by nearly all the English, especially the ones living in Ireland. The only consolation was all of Reid's tenants were very loyal and he already saw some of them arrive in wagons to come to their aid.

Despite everyone's efforts, the flames were quickly becoming uncontrollable. Reid's lungs burned from the smoke. It almost seemed like they were getting ahead but when he took a step back to take in the house, the west wing was enveloped. His gaze followed the building upward to the sky as he coughed.

"God, help us!" he cried out as hopelessness began to set in.

Reid was prepared to tell everyone to give up when he thought he felt a drop. He quickly glanced around to see if it was merely someone throwing yet another bucket of water and had spilled some near him. No one was there. He then glanced at the sky again to see, for the first time, that it was filled with thick clouds. There was another drop. Then another!

"Thank the Lord!" Reid sighed with exhaustion as it started to rain. It wasn't long before the others were hooting and jumping for joy. "The Lord has delivered us!" Reid shouted hoarsely.

"Reid, Reid!" He turned to see his mother running up to him.

"Mother, I'm so glad you're alright! Where is—"

"I don't know where Eibhleann and the baby are." The panicked tone in her voice hit him in the stomach with a sickening feeling.

"Aren't they with you?"

"No! I thought they were but…I searched within the group of women, who fled from the house. Reid, what if…." Elmira couldn't finish as she began to sob. Reid's vision immediately flooded with tears. He put his hand on his head and tried to gather his frantic thoughts. If Eibhleann and Rylan weren't with the women and nowhere in sight, it only meant one thing.

Reid took off running toward the front entrance. His staff did their best to try and stop him from going inside the now fragile and dangerous house. One footman even reached out and took hold of Reid's arm but he only pulled away. He raced to the front entrance. Reid grasped the door handle when he heard something like a faint cry. For a second, it sounded like it was coming from inside! Then he heard it again. It was Rylan's cry. Reid turned back to the yard and saw Eibhleann hurrying toward the small crowd. She was coming from the woods to the east of the house and was pushing a buggy. Reid now swiftly retraced his steps and rushed over to her.

"I thought you were…." he couldn't finish the horrible sentence. Instead he reached for Eibhleann and took her in his arms. By now they were both soaking wet from the rain but they didn't care. "I'm so glad you're all right."

"I'm so sorry!" Eibhleann cried, "We went for a walk then I saw the smoke…an' it started ter rain. I didn't realize how far we'd gone," she tried to explain before Reid kissed her.

It wasn't until then that Reid heard Rylan's cries. He and Eibhleann turned to see Elmira taking him out of the wet buggy to calm him. Reid was so overcome with joy that his family was safe. He embraced his wife again, thanking God over and over under his breath.

"Reid, you're hurt!" Eibhleann suddenly noticed the blood stains on his arm. Reid followed her gaze to his shirt, just as a twinge of pain came from it. It had been the last thing on his mind until then. As the adrenaline wore off, he began to feel lightheaded from the deep cut. "What happened?" Eibhleann asked in concern. Reid was about to answer her when he caught a glimpse of Elmira nearby.

"Not now. I'll tell you later."

"Alright but we must see to yer arm straight away," she admonished.

CHAPTER THIRTY-SIX

October 1821

$\mathscr{N}$early a month had passed and the rebuilding of Saerlaith's west wing was well underway. There hadn't been another attack of any kind. However, this didn't ease Reid's mind. He knew Garrick wasn't one to give up easily. Reid didn't want to wait around to see what his brother was planning next.

As soon as he made sure the building was going smoothly, he discussed it with Eibhleann then swiftly made plans to leave Ireland. He figured the Season and the sitting of parliament was fast approaching in the coming spring so it would be just as well to spend the winter in England. He was also pleased to have his mother accompany them. He was surprised at first but the fire had shaken Elmira up a bit. Reid hadn't mentioned anything to her about Garrick being behind the fire. Over the past few months after returning with Eibhleann from America, he had hinted about his brother but was shut down by Elmira. She couldn't grasp the thought that Garrick would harm anyone. At first, Reid himself had a hard time trying to understand it. How could Elmira's own son set fire to the house with her still inside. Upon further investigation days later, Reid found out from the gardener that when the men had come on their land with torches to start the fire, Elmira was safely in the garden, reading. Though, it happened so fast that Gregory McCline was unable to see any of their faces.

Nonetheless, Reid was very glad to be leaving. He dearly hoped things would calm down while they were away.

Roland entered the pub and hurriedly searched the room. *There he is,* he sighed with relief then made his way to Garrick. He sat alone at a table in the corner. Roland had already been to two other pubs before this one, looking everywhere for him.

Once he reached the table, he plopped down on the chair across from Garrick. He immediately leaned forward to keep his news exclusively between them.

"They left. I just saw Reid and his family get on a ship," Roland quietly informed. Garrick lowered his ale and wiped the foam from his lips with his sleeve.

"Running away is he?" Garrick chuckled gruffly.

"I stayed at the harbor and watched until the ship set sail.

Where do you think he's going?"

"Oh, I know where he's going. He's going to his fancy townhouse in London, no doubt. What were you doing at the harbor anyway?"

"I've been working some…here and there," Roland explained.

"What are you doing that for?" Garrick hiccupped, "I told you I had a job in mind for you."

"With all due respect, you don't appear to be a promising employer…wasting away in these pubs."

"Hey, it wasn't too long ago that I found you in this very one. I've merely been waiting for the right time. Sounds to me like the best time just presented itself," Garrick went on.

"For what?" Roland asked in hushed tones.

"Not here," Garrick stood and dropped a coin on the table. Roland followed his lead and stood as well. They then made their way out.

CHAPTER THIRTY-SEVEN

August 1822

"I wonder what that was all about?" Reid said once again as the carriage lurched forward.

"Dear, are ya sure it's not jist your imagination an' it's truly nothin'?" Eibhleann said as she lifted Rylan onto her lap.

"How else can you explain the strange behavior? Everyone ignored us the minute we stepped off the ship. I expect the English to spite us but not the Irish. Not one hello or friendly nod. This has never happened before, not since I helped them into parliament. Usually I can barely hold my bag because people come and offer to take it for me. You've seen when it happens. And another thing…did you notice how people stared at us and began to whisper to each other?" Reid asked in frustration.

"Well, nigh that you mention it. I did notice that,"

"Perhaps there's still talk of why we've been away so long," Elmira put in.

"That's probably it," Eibhleann agreed but she could tell Reid wasn't convinced. Just then they all caught sight of two men talking on the side of the road. When their carriage passed by, one of them pointed at it and appeared upset over something. "I tell you, something is going on!" Reid blurted. The women didn't say anything in hopes that he would calm down if they remained placid. It did little to help his anxiety. He was almost afraid of going home for what they might find once they arrived. *Garrick has done something,* the thought kept rolling around in Reid's mind. Though, he didn't say any more about it as the carriage left the harbor and started for Saerlaith.

They were more than halfway home when the driver suddenly spoke up from his place out front.

"My Lord, we're bein' flagged to stop by several horsemen…constables I think."

"What's going on?" Eibhleann and Elmira both asked as Reid instantly peered out of the window. Sure enough, several men in uniform rode up alongside them in order to stop them.

"Do as they say, Donald," Reid instructed and the carriage came to a halt.

"Reid, what do ya think they want?" Eibhleann put her hand on his arm in concern.

"It's probably some misunderstanding. I'll find out." With that, he went for the door.

"Can I help you sirs?" Reid emerged from the carriage and left the door open.

"Lord Kerrich, you are to come with us," a constable atop the horse in front of the others, stated.

"For what reason?"

"You must be brought before the magistrate, straight away."

"Whatever for? I've just returned from a long journey by ship and only wish to return home. Can't this wait until tomorrow at least?"

"Our orders are to be carried out immediately," the officer persisted.

"What is this concerning? Is it some land dispute?" Reid asked further.

"We are not to discuss it with you...only the magistrate. But I assure you, it is of the utmost seriousness and importance. All I can tell you is that it concerns the law."

"This is preposterous! I'm a member of peerage and also of parliament. I simply claim Privilege of Peerage on my behalf," Reid expressed confidently.

"That pardon is unable to exclude you from this matter." Upon hearing this, Reid turned and saw his wife peering out of the door. He met her worried look. The pardon he had just stated, granted him freedom from nearly every crime he could ever be accused of, except very few horrible acts such as murder.

"Surely you have the wrong information," he returned his gaze to the constable and said, almost in a whisper.

"You will have to take it up with the magistrate. Now you can come with us willingly or forcibly. The choice is yours." Reid had no choice but to oblige. He took a step forward to leave when he felt a hand on his arm.

"Reid." By now Eibhleann had climbed out of the carriage also. Her eyes were filled with fear.

"Don't worry. Everything will be alright once I get this straightened out. Have Donald bring the carriage for me once he brings you home. I will see you at home in no time." Husband and wife quietly separated and Reid was taken away. Eibhleann felt completely helpless as she watched them until they were out of sight. It couldn't be real. This couldn't be happening.

"What do we do? There must be something that can be done to stop this monstrosity!" It wasn't until Eibhleann heard Elmira that she forced herself to remove her gaze from the road.

"Perhaps...but what? We can't stay 'ere. We must go 'ome

as Reid said, I suppose," Eibhleann replied.

"I don't know what we could do…we can't just do nothing!" Elmira's anxious ranting and questions continued as Eibhleann climbed back inside. Eibhleann felt like she was in some sort of befuddled daze. However, the moment she sat down, it hit her. It seemed like a light suddenly kindled inside her.

"We can do one thin'," she blurted in assurance.

"What?" Elmira gasped.

"We can pray."

Once Rylan had gone down for a nap, Eibhleann went to one of the many guestrooms. She pulled a chair closer to the window that overlooked the road. This would give her an excellent view to know the moment Reid returned and also a quiet place to pray.

Her concerns had doubled since returning home without her husband. On the way to Saerlaith, Eibhleann saw something very strange. Two homes, belonging to their tenants, appeared to be badly burned. When she saw the first one, she figured it was some kind of accident but when the second destroyed home came into view, it caused her heart to sink into the pit of her stomach. There had to be a connection between the burned homes and Reid being taken to the magistrate.

But what could it be? Questions poured through her mind. Waiting was worst of all.

Eibhleann remained glued to her place next to the window for hours. Dinner was almost upon them before she finally saw any sign of her husband. The moment she spotted the carriage, she breathlessly hurried to the Great Hall.

"What 'appened? Did ye clear the matter up? What did they want?" Reid opened the door and was met with questions. Eibhleann grew silent as soon as she saw the solemn look on his face. He took off his hat and coat with a heavy sigh. In truth, he was trying to keep it together to not frighten or upset Eibhleann but it was too late for that. She took Reid's strained silence as a sign that something was terribly wrong.

"He has done it. Garrick has done the unthinkable," Reid breathed and hung his head.

"What 'as he done?" Eibhleann asked in a whisper and approached him. Reid gently pulled away from her embrace. He had to move to a chair and sit down before he could speak.

"The magistrate said," he gulped, "I've been charged with arson and…." he couldn't go on. He couldn't say it. It was too awful to think of much less speak of it or reveal to his wife.

Eibhleann instantly pictured the burned houses she saw upon returning home.

"They can't think that yer did these things. We weren't even in Ireland at the time," she lowered herself to kneel before Reid. "What wud ya gain by doin' such a thin'? We love an' care for the tenants loike they were our own family!"

"Eibhleann," Reid took her hands and gazed at her deeply. "I'm charged with arson…and murder." Saying it brought tears to both of them.

"What!" Eibhleann cried in disbelief.

"Old man Donovan, McCarthy…the young Whelan girl," Reid choked before he broke down completely and covered his face in his hands. "They're gone…dead…." Eibhleann embraced his trembling shoulders. It was as if they were in some kind of nightmare. "Why? Because they're Irish? Because they were my tenants?" he went on painfully, "I thought going to England was the right thing to do to remain safe. I thought Garrick would relent once he found out we had left. But now my decision has proved to be worse than I could have ever imagined." Hearing the sorrow in her husband's voice was unbearable.

"Did you tell them aboyt yer brather an' all he's done an' that he's the one behind this?" Eibhleann inquired and wiped her eyes.

"Yes! The magistrate wouldn't hear of it. Even when I told him I was in England and could prove what I said to be true."

"What did he say 'appened?" she asked again.

"He said my steward, Roland Carver and other men went to my tenants, one by one, and told them they were behind in rent so I had commanded them to be dealt with."

"You dismissed Roland long ago! Surely they must nu that."

"Yet they don't. I dismissed him quietly to not make more talk or scandal about our family. And no one knows where he is," Reid explained, growing more upset.

"The tenants 'ill stan' up for us, ter be sure. They nu ya wouldn't chucker anythin' like this!" Eibhleann's voice wavered.

"Will they?" Reid stood and went to the window, "I saw two of the homes that were burned, coming home. I also saw Mr. Whelan and his family cleaning up. He saw me as well. The moment he did, he turned his back on me. No one is with us," he sighed hopelessly.

"There is One who 'ill never forsake us," Eibhleann again approached him. "What 'appens nigh?"

"Because I'm a peer, the charge is sent to the Grand Jury and the case will be brought before the court at the King's Bench at the House of Lords. The Lord High Steward will preside but the entire house will be able to decide the ruling."

"But we jist returned from London," Eibhleann said.

"I have to, either willingly or forcibly."

"You can't! It 'ill be impossible for you ter git a fair trial. Everyone in the House av Lords 'ill be against ya."

"I'm afraid you're right. And the twenty Irishmen? They'll surely be against me because of the Irish who have died. I'm a member of peerage so I must be tried by them," Reid leaned against the windowsill and rubbed his face as the grim outlook settled in. The ruling would clearly be a death sentence. Of this he could be sure even before the trial was upon him. He could only think of how pleased the members of parliament would be once they heard of this. They had hated Reid for years and would be delighted to finally be rid of him.

"Whaen?" was all Eibhleann could ask.

"Tomorrow morning. The authorities will be here to escort me to the ship."

"I'm goin' with ya."

"No! What about the baby? The journey will be too much for you after just returning," Reid argued.

"No it won't. I'll brin' Rylan along. The townhouse 'ill be readily sufficient. I can't let ya face this alone. I won't!"

"They'll never let you into the courtroom."

"I know. You'll nade al' the support yer can git," Eibhleann stood her ground.

"I can't bear to let you come and see me being treated like a criminal. What if the ruling is…." He couldn't say it but Eibhleann knew what he meant. "I'm afraid of what they might do to you if…."

"Ya mustn't speak this way. I refuse ter allow us to prepare for the worst. We're stronger than that, wi' His 'elp. Reid, ya alwus say God is wi' us in trouble, to deliver us."

CHAPTER THIRTY-EIGHT

"*T*hey're here, My Lord," the butler informed. Reid had just finished saying goodbye to his tearful mother. He turned to the open door and took in the dreary escort. He then felt Eibhleann take his hand and squeeze it reassuringly.

They were about to go through the door when Eli came in from outside. Reid stopped to shake hands with his steward.

"You'll do fine in my absence once again," Reid encouraged, "The main thing is to regain the tenant's trust like we talked about last night."

"Thank you. I wish I could do more. Perhaps I could have done somethin' differently before, to have stopped all this," Eli revealed the regret that weighed heavily on him.

"Don't blame yourself. No one could have known this would happen. You've been more than loyal to me in many ways," Reid replied.

"Is there anything I can do? Anythin' at all?" Eli asked.

"Lord Kerrich, we must be going," one of the constables announced after he dismounted and neared the entrance.

"Yes, yes," Reid nodded to him. He then turned back to Eli, "Find Garrick!" he didn't have any time to say more as he, Eibhleann, Rylan, and a few other staff, walked to the carriage. It was surrounded by open buggies and a handful of officers.

The constable was about to lead Reid away from his family to a horse of his own.

"My family is coming with me to England. They will be following us in our carriage and the second will hold the staff. Might I ride with them as you escort all of us to the ship?" The constable hesitated at Reid's question. He moved his gaze to Eibhleann then to the carriages.

"Alright," he finally agreed.

Reid glanced back at Saerlaith one last time. He had to constantly fight the thought of never returning. Of never seeing his mother again or his tenants to tell them how sorry he was about all of this.

They probably never want to see me again anyway.

"Reid, don't," Eibhleann spoke up and cut into his sad musings. Reid glanced at her. "I nu what yer must be feelin' but don't allow the doubts to rise up in ya nor your thoughts to dwell on the wrong things." Reid could tell she was doing all she could to not break down herself.

"I'm so glad you're with me. I couldn't do this alone," he admitted. Before she could catch herself, a tear slid down her cheek as Reid lovingly touched her face.

CHAPTER THIRTY-NINE

September 1822

here are they taking me? Reid asked himself in confusion when he passed the door he thought he was being led to. Instead, he was taken further down the hall inside Westminster Palace.

He kept his thoughts to himself, that is until they stopped in front of a large set of double doors.

"Why are we here? This is the—" Reid stopped in mid-sentence when he glanced at the two guards. They simply looked back at him but didn't appear as if they cared or planned to answer him anyway. *What's the point of asking them? They're only following orders.*

The guards opened the doors and Reid was shown into the Lords Chamber. He was astonished to find every one of the red benches filled with nearly every member of the House of Lords. Because parliament wasn't in session and the London Season was behind them, Reid would normally be tried in the Court of the Lord High Steward, where the steward would choose about twelve peers to act as Lord Triers. Reid was prepared for a small group of men in the smaller court but not this. Even if they used the Lord's Chamber, he couldn't figure out how all these men were still in town. This was unheard of. Howbeit, Reid could do nothing about it.

As Reid humbly walked to the stand, the truth slowly dawned on him.

Word certainly got out about what happened and the charges. Everyone must have been summoned or told to come one way or another. They deliberately came to ensure I would be rid of. Deep down he had wondered if the members of peerage might try something unscrupulous. The glares seemed to weigh down on him. He could feel how much they detested him. The animosity seemed to fill the air.

When he reached his spot, Reid got enough courage to glance up to meet the stares. He searched out the Irishmen he'd help get there. Each man wore a solemn frown and had stubbornly set their jaw, telling him, he would find no mercy from them. Reid felt betrayed, especially since each man had treated him completely different only months before. They had revered him as a hero, as did everyone in Ireland before all of this.

Reid wasn't prepared to meet this. Everyone in the room was against him and they would be the very ones to decide if he lived or died. As much as he tried finding some hope or faith to help him, every thought was that of defeat and hopelessness. It was as if he was falling and couldn't get a footing on anything.

All the preliminary ceremonies began but Reid hardly noticed what was being said. It wasn't until he heard his name that he was brought back to attention.

"Lord Kerrich, we all know why you are here and of the charges," the Lord High Steward stated in a monotone voice. Though it held a bit of pompousness, he spoke as if it meant nothing and it was just an ordinary, mundane task. It made anger rise up in Reid how he acted when his very life was at stake! "I don't see why we need to drag this on any longer than absolutely necessary, especially since we're not officially in session.

I'm sorry my case is taking up your precious time! Reid was furious and could barely keep silent. *I don't want to be here either.* However, he knew better. Not one of these members would choose to be anywhere else at that moment. Not when such a fine opportunity had presented itself.

"I don't see why we can't have this matter cleared up in less than a few days. Let us begin."

Eibhleann had brought some knitting for the wait out in the hall, yet over an hour had passed and she still hadn't touched it. All she could do was pray and flinch every time a door opened and she thought it might be Reid. Most of the time however, was spent in pushing aside fearful thoughts.

Eibhleann's gaze shot up and she gasped when Reid finally emerged. There were three men that came with him. She stood but didn't go to him right away, for the men spoke quietly with him. She wanted so badly to ask how it went yet now wasn't the time. When Reid did break away and approached, he spoke formally.

"We can go back to our townhouse now. They'll allow me to stay with you there as long as two guards remain at the entrance." Eibhleann nodded then they were off.

Reid remained silent until they were alone in their carriage and on their way home. After he ended his business-like resolve, he leaned forward and rubbed his face in his hands.

"What went on in there?" Eibhleann asked, her voice was barely more than a whisper.

"Oh Eibhleann…I can't do this! Every last one of them are against me. They'll happily see me hang!" The moment he said the word, Eibhleann gasped. Tears stung her eyes and her breath caught in her throat at his brashness. "I don't want to lose you," he cried.

"Don't lose 'ope. Ya can't!" she choked and tried to come up with something encouraging to tell him.

"I'm sorry," Reid's voice was filled with emotion as he finally met her gaze, crying. She had never seen him undone and this upset before. It frightened her.

Eibhleann meekly slipped off her seat and moved to be next to him.

"I'm sorry for everything," he blurted before they wept in each other's arms, overwhelmed with grief.

CHAPTER FORTY

lessed be God, even the Father of our Lord Jesus Christ, the Father of mercies, and the God of all comfort;

⁴ Who comforteth us in all our tribulation, that we may be able to comfort them which are in any trouble, by the comfort wherewith we ourselves are comforted of God.

⁵ For as the sufferings of Christ abound in us, so our consolation also aboundeth by Christ.

⁶ And whether we be afflicted, it is for your consolation and salvation, which is effectual in the enduring of the same sufferings which we also suffer: or whether we be comforted, it is for your consolation and salvation.

7 And our hope of you is stedfast, knowing, that as ye are partakers of the sufferings, so shall ye be also of the consolation.

8 For we would not, brethren, have you ignorant of our trouble which came to us in Asia, that we were pressed out of measure, above strength, insomuch that we despaired even of life:

9 But we had the sentence of death in ourselves, that we should not trust in ourselves, but in God which raiseth the dead:

10 Who delivered us from so great a death, and doth deliver: in whom we trust that he will yet deliver us.

Eibhleann awoke from her horrible dream. She quickly glanced over to Reid's side of the bed to assure it was only a dream and he safely lay beside her. She instantly became alarmed when he wasn't there!

Oh no! What if? Eibhleann quickly sat up then caught a glimpse of a light coming from the small private sitting room, right off the bedroom. *Thank goodness,* she breathed a sigh of relief.

She quietly slipped out of bed and went to the open door. Reid was kneeling against the couch with his head bent in prayer. His Bible lay open beside him. Eibhleann didn't want to disturb him so she retraced her steps back to the bed and lay back down against her pillow. She gazed up at the ceiling. Tears tempted to come again as the same worrisome thoughts came over her. This time however, she chose to fight it. Worrying and fretting over the serious situation would solve nothing. By giving into them, she was slowly realizing that they were accepting defeat before the ruling was even final.

"Lord, please forgive us. Forgive us for not puttin' our trust in You…the only One who can deliver us from this. I don't nu how but I trust You." Unbeknown to Eibhleann, Reid's prayer was exactly the same as hers. After finally giving up trying to fall asleep, Reid got his Bible out and went to the sitting room. That's where he stumbled upon Second Corinthians. The verses in the first chapter covered his troubling situation so perfectly that Reid was taken aback. The apostle Paul had expressed what Reid was experiencing at that moment, although, he responded to the tribulation differently. Instead of giving in to the problems, Paul chose not to trust in himself but God, who is the God of all comfort. He was thoroughly convinced that God would deliver him. Reid instantly saw the difference between his own response and what Paul did. Reid now knew the change he had to make before God could come to his aid.

Without letting one more second pass, Reid set down the open Bible, slid off the couch to his knees to pray. He began with asking for forgiveness for doubting and not trusting God to deliver him. He stayed there for the remainder of the night.

Eibhleann continued to seek the Lord as well. She must have eventually fallen off to sleep because the next thing she knew was waking up that morning. She opened her eyes to find Reid bent over her to kiss her forehead.

"Oh, are ya leavin'?" she asked.

"I didn't mean to wake you. I must be on my way."

"Is it that time already?" Eibhleann sat up.

"It's alright," Reid replied.

"I so wanted ter go with ya."

"You can still come once you're ready," he reassured her then sat down on the edge of the bed beside her. "Before I leave, I must apologize."

"Ya don't nade to—"

"I have to. I'm sorry for leading you…both of us, astray by not trusting God to help us as I should have from the very start. I was so consumed with what might happen that I very nearly lost my faith. I had forgotten all the previous times He has delivered us. I see now that this is the Lord's fight. He's my Father and as that role, He'll fight this case. All I need to do is trust Him…to say what He wants me to say and do what He has me do. I meet this today with renewed hope and purpose."

"I'm so relieved. I wus guilty av this as well," Eibhleann admitted.

"I love you. See you soon," Reid lovingly caressed Eibhleann's stray hair in her face then got up to leave.

By the time Eibhleann arrived, the court was already in session. She waited in the hall until they took a short break for lunch. Eibhleann was notified that Reid had been taken to a different room and was asking for her.

"Dear, how are ya farin'? What wus said in there?" Eibhleann asked once she entered and sat down at the small table where Reid's food sat untouched.

"Well, they're saying the fact that I wasn't even in Ireland, and that I had fired Roland Carver months before this happened, doesn't amount to any proof that I wasn't behind it," Reid solemnly explained. Eibhleann could hear the frustration in his voice. "They also said not one of our tenants wish to speak in my defense. They seem to think I should have told everyone the moment I dismissed Roland. Perhaps I should have. I only wanted to keep things quiet and not make it worse. I have no other proof because Garrick and Roland have both disappeared," he sighed. "They won't hear anything I tell them." Eibhleann put her hand on his shoulder, as if to remind him of their conversation just that morning.

"I feel like David when he stood before the giant. But he considered God much greater than Goliath. I purpose to do the same, even if it's not easy." Reid looked at Eibhleann with a renewed sense of courage.

"An' I as well."

Later that afternoon, Reid and several men emerged from the courtroom much like the previous day. This time however, when Reid came over to Eibhleann, who stood up from her place in the hall, two men accompanied him. Eibhleann glanced up at Reid in question.

"They said they've heard all they need. The sentencing will be tomorrow morning. They seem to think I might try to leave London tonight so I have to be taken into custody until then."

"What? Ya 'aven't shown them any call ter think you'll resist or try to flee." Anger instantly aroused in Eibhleann.

"I know. I tried to tell them." Reid felt for his wife as he watched her struggle to accept it.

"I'll see you the'morra then," her voice trembled. She then meekly kissed him.

"I love you," Reid whispered.

"I love yer," she hugged him before he was taken away.

CHAPTER FORTY-ONE

t's time." Reid looked up at the guard, who had opened the door to the small room. He got to his feet and silently followed. He was led down the long hall and into the noisy courtroom.

As soon as everyone spotted Reid when he entered, they quieted down almost immediately. Reid felt everyone's eyes on him as he stepped behind the stand. Some of the members of the house, who were intently watching Reid, were surprised for they could find no fear on his countenance.

"Court is now in session," the Lord High Steward announced. "Lord Kerrich," his cold tone echoed in the vast room. Reid forced himself to meet his unfriendly stare. He could hear is own heart beating loudly as he awaited his fate. The place was so quiet that Reid's nervous breathing toned out everything around him making it seem like he was the only one in the court.

It felt like forever before the lord looked up from the papers on his podium and went on with the sentencing.

"You are free to go."

"Wha...what?" Reid blinked in confusion. Rustling and whispers came from the crowd of men, on the benches on either side of Reid.

"Evidence has been found, moments ago, causing the charges to be dropped. You are free to go." the Lord High Steward's voice was as tedious as ever. He appeared quite disappointed by this new finding.

"How can this—" Reid began but he cut him off by pounding his wooden gavel on the stand loudly.

"Court is adjourned."

Eibhleann watched the door diligently, waiting to find out the results of the ruling. She didn't really know how long it would take. When the door finally swung open Eibhleann flinched. She then watched the men pour out of the courtroom. She couldn't tell what the sentence might be by the sullen look on their faces. Eibhleann slowly got to her feet as she tried to locate Reid among them.

"Eibhleann!" someone called her name. She looked around the busy hall. "Eibhleann!" Reid suddenly came through the men, rushed up to her, and took her in his arms.

"What 'appened? What is the rulin'?" she eventually pulled

away to hear the answer.

"I'm free! I'm free to go!"

"What? How?"

"I don't even know. The Lord has showed Himself faithful! He has delivered us!" Reid rejoiced.

"But I...don't understand!" "Eibhleann tried to process what he'd just said.

"I don't either. It's a miracle! They wouldn't tell me the details."

"You're free? We can go 'um!" It seemed to finally sink in and she expressed her joy!

"There you are," a man spoke right behind Eibhleann. They both quickly turned to see who it was.

"Eli? What are you doing here?" Reid asked in astonishment.

EPILOGUE

July 1822

 usk was upon them as Garrick and Roland rode up to the home of the Flynn's. They stopped right outside the front door when Roland opened his mouth to speak, as was the plan.

"Wait, not yet," Garrick whispered to him.

"What do you mean not yet? You told me to!"

"I'm going to start the house on fire first. Then you can go on with your speech," Garrick went on to explain as he dismounted.

"You never said that! What if they can't get everyone out in time?" Roland asked nervously.

"I don't care if every one of these Irish bogtrotters die!"

"Garrick, there are small children inside! Our agreement was to set their homes on fire only to scare them. I never agreed to kill anyone!" Roland's voice was becoming increasingly louder in his frantic state.

"Just hush before you ruin the entire thing. Save your whining for someone else," Garrick ignored the former steward's upset whispers and set fire to the thatched roof.

When they heard screams coming from inside, Garrick turned to Roland and motioned the go ahead. Before Roland could start, the front door burst open and the panicked family began to scramble to get everyone out. The roof burst into flames almost instantly.

"Because you are behind in rent, Lord Kerrich has instructed to have you dealt with until he is paid in full!" Roland had to shout over the family's coughing and yelling.

The plan had been successfully carried out so Garrick climbed back onto his horse and took off.

"Come on!" he shouted back to Roland, who seemed to be in some kind of stupor.

What have I gotten myself into? Roland fearfully asked himself. Because he feared Garrick, he reluctantly followed him.

They silently rode on into the night. By now they'd visited three homes and were now on their way to the fourth. Roland couldn't get the distraught faces of the tenants, nor their screams out of his mind. He couldn't go through with this. Roland now knew what Garrick had been planning all along but he couldn't swallow it. He hated the Irish just as much as most of the other

English but not enough to kill them in their beds. He had to stop this!

Roland went back and forth in his mind until enough courage rose up in him to act.

"I want no more of this!" Roland stated boldly and came to a halt. Garrick just kept riding. "Do you hear me? You can't do this without me. I'm finished!" he shouted again. Garrick eventually turned his horse and approached.

"You agreed to this…for payment! You are going to finish this tonight," he spewed in anger.

"I never agreed to have people killed. You could be hanged for this if the authorities find out!" Garrick saw the idea come to Roland just then, to tell them himself.

"Not if I kill you first," his simple and heartless threat shocked the former steward.

So that's it then. Do as he says or be killed. The hate and contempt in Garrick's eyes smothered any courage Roland had left.

"We have to hurry before all of Ireland finds out what we're doing," Garrick said and urged his horse along. Roland had no choice but to follow.

Roland waited for the signal and watched Garrick sneak up to the side of the house with the torch.

"Who are ya an' what will ya bea 'avin' to do with me?" Out of nowhere, someone shouted. A man, holding a rifle, must have come out of the shed to the left of the house. He walked up to Roland with a lad beside him and now stood between Roland and the house where Garrick was. Roland's gaze quickly looked behind the father and son to see where he was but he was nowhere to be found.

Must be hiding behind the house.

"I say, what do ya want?" the Irishman asked again. He held up his rifle to show he meant business.

"Ah yes…it's me…Roland Carver. Lord Kerrich's steward," he lied. It was then that he saw Garrick rush up behind the man. The man opened his mouth to speak when he was swiftly hit over the head with the other end of the torch. He was out cold.

"We have to get out of here!" Roland began to panic.

"Not before we finish this." Garrick rushed back to the house and lit the roof.

"The plan is already ruined! Too much has gone wrong." While the two men started to quarrel, they didn't notice the boy scramble to the house to get everyone out. The building was ablaze in seconds.

"We're not done! We've only begun with these four. There are many more!" Garrick was about to run to his horse where Roland held the reigns from his place on his steed.

"No. I'm through with you. You've gone too far!" Roland dropped the reigns to Garrick's horse and shooed the animal away. He would now be stranded. Roland knew Garrick couldn't continue on with the plan without him, much less without his horse. Roland then clicked his horse, turning his back on the fuming Garrick, and was off.

Garrick would not put up with this. He went to the unconscious man and picked up the rifle he had dropped. He held it up in Roland's direction and pulled the trigger. Roland fell off his steed and lay unmoving.

"Bloody fool," Garrick said through clenched teeth. Now the plan was surely ruined. He was now without a horse as well. After Roland fell to the ground, his steed ran off. All of a sudden, he heard his own horse neigh. It was coming from behind the house. Garrick turned back to the house to see where it was when another shot was heard. Roland had used all the strength he had left to reach for his own gun and shoot Garrick in the back, causing him to fall forward and into the inferno.

August 1822

Eli and fifteen men rode into the yard of the Whelan family. Eli had just climbed down from his horse when Mr. Whelan came out of the shed, which doubled as his family's makeshift shelter since their home had been burned.

"What do yer want?" he spitefully asked. Eli figured as much. The previous burned home they had gone to had started out the same. The tenants hated their landlord and everyone under him since the fires. Just as Reid had instructed, Eli would try to smooth things over, that is, if Mr. Whelan would allow him to do so. This matter would be a bit more fragile than the last because Mr. Whelan's daughter had perished that night.

"We've come to clean up and help build a new house for you."

"An' why wud ya do that...since ya burned it in the first place," Mr. Whelan held his rifle tightly.

"I know what everyone thinks happened. I'm not here to argue...just to lend a hand," Eli said calmly.

"Why doesn't Lord Kerrich face me 'imself instead av 'eadin' raun loike a coward and havin' others deal wi' his tenants?" he spouted angrily.

"As I said, we're only here to help, if you'll allow us to."

"Can't stop ya," Whelan turned to go back to his own work. Eli turned to his men and nodded to them. They all in turn, dismounted to begin working.

A few hours had passed and they were all still at work, cleaning up. Eli wiped the sweat from his brow and lifted another burned beam. It was only then that something caught his eye. The tiny item in the ashes sparkled in the sunlight.

What is that? he bent over and found a ring. *Must belong to the Whelan's...but it's very grand....* All of a sudden Eli recalled when they had found Garrick and his men camped out near Saerlaith. *Reid had taken the very ring from his brother's hand. Then he threw it back to him. It can only mean one thing!*

"Mr. McConahay." Eli heard someone call to him. Eli closed his grip on the ring and turned to Saerlaith's footman.

"Yes, what is it?" Eli asked.

"Wallace and I...we rode into town to get more building supplies but we took a shortcut through the woods," Stuart pointed to the trees behind them. "We came upon a body," he explained in all seriousness, "It's Roland Carver, sir."

That's why no one could find either of them. Urgency rose up in Eli. *I have to get to England!*

September 1822

The Lord High Steward took his seat at the head of the courtroom. He then turned to his page, who stood nearby, ready to assist.

"We're about ready. Send for Lord Kerrich—" Before the words had been fully spoken, the doors to the room opened loudly and a man walked in. The lord peered over the high podium to find a young man. By the looks of his plain clothes, he was not a member of the House of Lords.

How did he get in here? he thought. "Who are you and why have you come to disrupt this session?" the Lord High Steward asked in annoyance. Eli boldly held up Garrick's ring.

"I have the necessary evidence to prove that Lord Kerrich is innocent!"

April 1823

Reid walked through the small crowd. He and Eibhleann had invited friends, family, and tenants to Saerlaith. They were all gathered in the garden where refreshments had been prepared. Reid was slowly making his way to the front, against the house. He mingled as he went, shaking hands and thanking everyone for coming to the small get-together. He soon found Eibhleann. She was talking with someone until she saw him approach. She smiled at him when he offered his arm to have her accompany him.

"If I could get everyone's attention please," Reid announced. He faced everyone dear to him and was swiftly reminded of what a fortunate and blessed man he was to have each of them in his life. As he slowly scanned the crowd, he caught sight of Elmira happily holding Rylan, Eli McConahay, Eibhleann's parents, the Whelan family, and other tenants, but not all.

"I'm so grateful for all of you that have come. Not all would but I believe with time, we will regain their trust. I thank God for each and every one of you. We shall remember this day as the day the Lord delivered us from all who were against us and for all He's done. We also remember and honor those who lost their lives." As he spoke, he saw many wipe their eyes. Reid was moved to tears himself during the long pause. Not only over the people who were no longer with them, but the greatness of God. God's love for them was overwhelming.

"All is not lost as we regain hope and renewed faith in our loving Father. Having said this, I'm brought back to scripture that has helped me through every difficulty," Reid pulled a small Bible out of his pocket and paged through it until he came upon the spot at the end of Romans chapter eight. "'What shall we then say to these things? If God be for us, who can be against us? He that spared not his own Son, but delivered him up for us all, how shall he not with him also freely give us all things? Who shall lay any thing to the charge of God's elect? It is God that justifieth. Who is he that condemneth? It is Christ that died, yea rather, that is risen again, who is even at the right hand of God, who also maketh intercession for us. Who shall separate us from the love of Christ? shall tribulation, or distress, or persecution, or famine, or nakedness, or peril, or sword? Nay, in all these things we are more than conquerors through him that loved us. For I am persuaded, that neither death, nor life, nor angels, nor principalities, nor powers, nor things present, nor things to come, Nor height, nor depth, nor any other creature, shall be able to separate us from the love of God, which is in Christ Jesus our Lord.'"

Kelly Aul lives in a small, rural town in Minnesota with her parents and two younger siblings. They were homeschooled which made their family very close. Growing up, Kelly had a very vivid imagination. She was always pretending, making up games with her siblings, and finding adventure around her home on a small lake. Kelly is enthralled with European history, especially the 19th century, writing, and most importantly the things of God. She is in fulltime ministry, along with her family,

Some people might be thinking, "Why do you have to mention God throughout this whole book? Dedication and everything?"

"Whatsoever ye do in word or deed, do all in the name of the Lord Jesus." (Colossians 3:17)

I can't stop talking about Him because He *is* my everything. And because He's my everything, God is in everything I do.

I've read some Christian novels, and it seems almost as if they try to go as close to the edge as they can and still call it a Christian book, but the question shouldn't be how close can I get before crossing the line. It should be, how close can I get to God? How much can I talk about Him? How can I give more glory to Him?

I don't ever want my readers to have to ask themselves, "Should I be reading this? Would God read this book? Could I read this book in front of my pastor or parents without guilt?"

Thank you for reading. I hope you enjoyed yourself and were inspired. And I have to say again, I give God all the glory for every part of this book. Without Him, I can do nothing.

— God bless, Kelly

Jesus said, except a man be born again, he cannot see the kingdom of God. (John 3:3) Being born again or the New Birth is not: confirmation, church membership, water baptism, being moral, doing good deeds.

Ephesians 2:8-9 "For by grace are ye saved through faith; and that not of yourselves: it is the gift of God: not of works, lest any man should boast."

You have to simply admit you are just what the Bible says — a lost sinner. Then you come and accept what Christ has purchased for you — a gift! (Romans 10:9-10)

Please pray this prayer to receive Jesus as your Savior.

Dear Heavenly Father, I believe in my heart that Jesus Christ is the Son of God, that He was crucified, died, and rose from the dead.

I ask you, Lord Jesus, to be Lord of my life. Thank you for saving me and coming into my heart, for forgiving me and redeeming me from all sin.

It's important to find a church where they teach the Word of God by studying right from the Bible, and to renew your mind by reading the Bible every day.

— Maggie Aul, Senior Pastor
Love of God Family Church
www.LoveofGodFamilyChurch.com

Kelly Aul

Spoiler Alert!

The Author recommends readers not to read beyond this point until they finish reading this book, Everlasting. There's nothing worse than ruining the mystery in the pages!

Family Tree

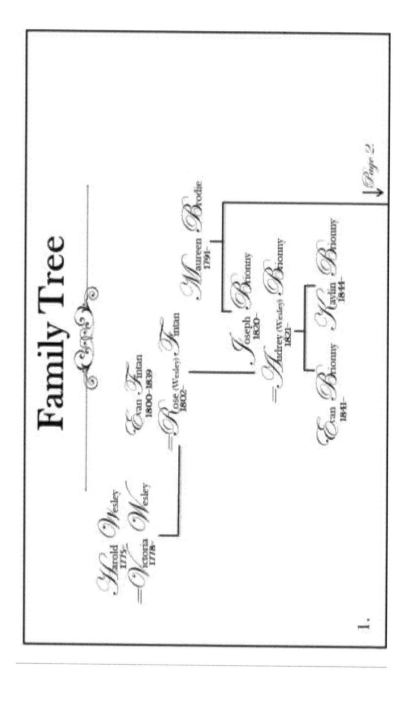

↓ Page 2

1.

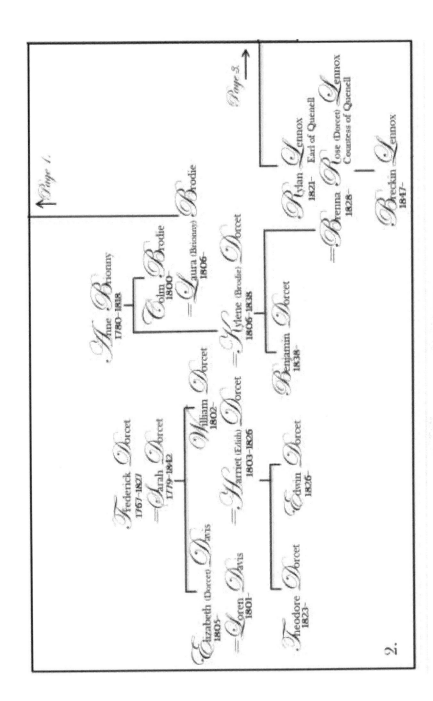

Page 3. →

Anne Brodny
1780–1818

Frederick Dorcet
1767–1827
=Sarah Dorcet
1779–1842

Colm Brodie
1800–
=Laura (Brennan) Brodie
1806–

William Dorcet
1802–

Elizabeth (Dorcet) Davis
1803–
=Loren Davis
1801–

Harriet (Edith) Dorcet
1803–1826

Kylene (Brodie) Dorcet
1805–1838

Benjamin Dorcet
1838–

Rylan Lennox
1821–
Earl of Quenell

Brenna (Dorcet) Lennox
1828–
Countess of Quenell

Edwin Dorcet
1826–

Theodore Dorcet
1823–

Breckin Lennox
1847–

2.

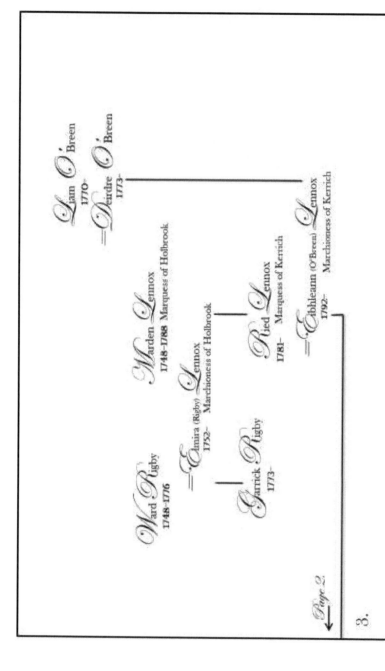

Liam O'Breen
1770–
=Deirdre O'Breen
1773–

Ward Rigby
1748–1776

Warden Lennox
1748–1788 Marquess of Holbrook
=Elmira (Rigby) Lennox
1752– Marchioness of Holbrook

Garrick Rigby
1773–

Ried Lennox
1781– Marquess of Kerrich
=Eibhleann (O'Breen) Lennox
1792– Marchioness of Kerrich

Page 2.

3.

1770		Ward Rigby marries Elmira
1772		John McNiel born
1773		Garrick Rigby born
1776		Ward Rigby dies in war
1779		Marden Lennox (Marquess of Cantrell) marries Elmira
1781		Reid Lennox born
1788		Marden Lennox dies
1800		Colm Brodie born
1801	August	Irish are granted into the House of Lords
1804		John McNiel marries Lenora
1805		John and Lenora McNiel have son, Dennon
	March	Reid Lennox meets Eibhleann O'Breen
1806		Kylene Brodie born
		Laura Brionny born
	April	Reid Lennox (Marquess of Kerrich) marries Eibhleann O'Breen
1808		Lenora McNiel goes to America with Dennon
		John McNiel goes after his wife and son once he saved enough money
		Dennon McNiel dies
1810		Maureen Brionny has miscarriage
1814		John McNiel gets a job with Princeton Shipping Company and eventually becomes Captain
1815		Maureen Brionny has son
	March	Eibhleann Lennox has baby but the child is stillborn

1815	September	Eibhleann Lennox meets Captain John McNeil
1816		Maureen Brionny's son dies
	April	Eibhleann Lennox leaves with Captain McNeil
	July	Reid Lennox finds his wife
1818		Colm and Kylene Brodie's Parents Die. They move to America
		Captain McNiel finds Pete (Lenora's Brother) and almost kills him - instead, Pete shoots McNiel in the leg
1820		Joseph Brionny born
	April	William Dorcet meets Kylene Brodie
	August	Captain McNiel throws Evan and Rose Fintan off of his ship, The St. Carlin
1821		Rylan Lennox born
		Audrey Wesley born
	August	Frederick Dorcet finds out about William's secret relationship with Kylene and breaks them apart.
	September	Saerlaith is set on fire
	October	William marries Harriet Edith
		Reid and Eibhleann Lennox leave Ireland and go to England
1822	July	Garrick Rigby and Roland Carver commit arson and murder
		Garrick Rigby dies
	August	Reid and Eibhleann Lennox return to Saerlaith
	September	Reid is found innocent

1823		William and Harriet have a son, Theodore Dorcet
1826		William and Harriet have a son, Edwin Dorcet
	May	Frederich Dorcet has heart attack
	July	Harriet Dorcet dies
1827	May	Frederick Dorcet dies
		Colm Brodie is offered job in Ireland after his uncle dies. Colm and Kylene plan to return to Ireland
	August	William finds and marries Kylene Brodie - Colm goes to Ireland alone
1828		Brenna Rose Dorcet born
1833		Man comes to buy Brionny land
		Joseph Brionny's father dies
		Famine comes to Ireland and Joseph gets a job on ship
1834		Colm Brodie marries Laura Brionny
1835	March	Brionny's house is started on fire with Maureen and Laura inside
1838	June	Joseph Brionny comes home and thinks his family died in fire
	August	Joseph gets a job on The St. Carlin
	November	William and Kylene have a son, Benjamin Dorcet
1839		After searching for the shell for eighteen years, Captain McNiel kidnapps Audrey Wesley
		Joseph Brionny meets Audrey Wesley
	July	Captain McNiel dies in storm

1839	August	Brenna gets to London, England
	September	Audrey comes home
		Lanna Ryan goes to Cheverell's for The London Season
	November	Lanna meets Stephen Kinsey
1840	July	Joseph Brionny marries Audrey Wesley
		Lanna marries Stephen Kinsey
1841	June	Joseph and Audrey have a son, Evan Brionny
	October	Stephen and Lanna have a son, Tully Kinsey
1842		Stephen and Lanna take in Brenna Dorcet
		Stephen and Lanna have a daughter, Audrey Kinsey
1844	April	Joseph and Audrey have a daughter, Kalin Brionny
	May	Brenna meets Rylan Lennox, Earl of Quenell
	July	Jake Harper marries Rose Wesley
1845	March	Rylan marries Brenna
	May	Brenna has dream about wheat
	August	The Blight
1846	August	The second Blight
1847	May	Rylan and Brenna have a son, Breckin Lennox
	June	Joseph Brionny finds his mother and sister
		Brenna finds her family

- ❖ Pronunciation of Eibhlcann ~ Avelynn
- ❖ Pronunciation of Saerlaith ~ ser-la

❖ Please visit the Official Author Website
www.kellyaul.com

❖ Like on Facebook
facebook.com/NeverForsakenBookSeries

NEVER FORSAKEN ~ BOOK ONE

She knows nothing of the tragedy that haunts her family's past.

Audrey has had enough of the emptiness of society and prays for something more. Unbeknown to her, someone is watching her every move just waiting for the right moment. It's only when Audrey faces death that her faith proves true at all costs in the midst of the storm. A new beginning is finally able to transpire when all is revealed and love is found in the most unlikely place.

AUDREY'S SUNRISE BOOK PREVIEW
Check out the video!
http://youtu.be/mrgABZLImjc

NEVER FORSAKEN ~ BOOK TWO

She is held captive within herself with no chance of being rescued.

One decision changed their family forever. One choice tore them apart. Their every thought is now consumed with regret.

When everything she holds dear is taken away, her faith dwindles to nothing. She has no choice but to resign herself to the sorrowful fact that her once childlike faith in God, was nothing more than that...childish.

It isn't long before something else discovers her vulnerable state. She doesn't know what it is until it's too late. There is no one to turn to and the dreadful grips of fear, that haunts her every move, is hers alone to endure.

Try as she might to hide away her past completely, her persistent dreams won't let her forget. She's tempted to give in to the black shadows and simply give up.

She soon finds herself desperately searching for the one place she never wanted to see again. It is where she comes upon a treasure. Something that holds her only rescue from the dark presence pursuing her, as she finds hope in the midst of darkness.

IN THE MIDST OF DARKNESS BOOK PREVIEW
Check out the video!

http://youtu.be/0FeHG-E06OQ

NEVER FORSAKEN ~ BOOK THREE

She must hold onto a hope when everything around her is falling away.

Brenna had lost everything dear to her. She had little else to do but come to the end of herself. At her darkest moment, an unexpected lifeline was shown her. Will she be able to hold fast to it as overwhelming challenges come upon her? Fear tempted to rise up in her. She couldn't help but wonder if the trying matter would awaken everything she had finally been able to rid herself from.

When a challenge far beyond her wildest dreams befalls her, Brenna truly sees she must let go of her mere efforts and cling to God completely. The power of love and faith she discovers is unshakable.

HOLDING FAITH BOOK PREVIEW
Check out the video!

http://youtu.be/0LShVcjJOVY

Made in the USA
Middletown, DE
07 August 2016